THE PYRAMID OF MUD

It's been raining for days in Vigàta, and the persistent downpours have led to violent floods overtaking Inspector Montalbano's beloved hometown. It is on one of these endless grey days that a man, a Mr Giugiù Nicotra, is found dead, his body discovered in a large water main with a bullet in his back. The investigation is slow and slippery to start with, but when the inspector realizes that every clue he uncovers and every person he interviews is leading to the same place — the world of public spending, and with it, the Mafia — the case begins to pick up pace. But there's one question that keeps playing on Montalbano's mind: in his strange and untimely death, was Giugiù Nicotra trying to tell him something?

THE PYRAMID
OF MUD

ANDREA CAMILLERI

TRANSLATED BY STEPHEN SARTARELLI

LARGE
PRINT

First published in Great Britain 2018
by
Mantle
an imprint of Pan Macmillan

First Isis Edition
published 2018
by arrangement with
Pan Macmillan

Originally published in Italian in 2014 as
La piramide di fango by Sellerio Editore, Palermo.

A catalogue record for this book is available
from the British Library.

ISBN 978–1–78541–582–1 (hb)
ISBN 978–1–78541–588–3 (pb)

Published by
F. A. Thorpe (Publishing)
Anstey, Leicestershire

Set by Words & Graphics Ltd.
Anstey, Leicestershire
Printed and bound in Great Britain by
T. J. International Ltd., Padstow, Cornwall

This book is printed on acid-free paper

CHAPTER
ONE

The thunderclap was so loud that not only did Montalbano suddenly wake up in terror, but he gave such a start that he nearly fell out of bed.

For over a week it had been raining cats and dogs without a moment's pause. The heavens had opened and seemed to have no intention of closing ever again.

It was raining not only in Vigàta, but all over Italy. In the north the rivers were bursting their banks and doing incalculable damage, and in a few towns the inhabitants had to be evacuated. But it was no joke in the south, either. Rivers and streams that had been dry for years and given up for dead had come back to life with a vengeance and broken loose, ravaging homes and farmlands.

The previous evening, the inspector had heard a scientist say on television that all of Italy was in danger of suffering a gigantic geological disaster, because it had never had a government willing to undertake any serious maintenance of the land. In short, it was as if a homeowner had never taken the trouble to repair a leaky roof or damaged foundations, and then was surprised and complained when one day his house collapsed on top of him.

Maybe this is exactly what we deserve, Montalbano thought bitterly.

He turned on the light and looked at his watch. Six-oh-five. Too early to get out of bed.

He lay there with eyes closed, listening to the crashing of the sea. Whether calm or in a frenzy, the sound of it always gave him pleasure. Then it suddenly dawned on him that the rain had stopped. He got out of bed and opened the shutters.

The thunderclap had been like the big boom that marks the end of a fireworks display. Indeed, there was no more water falling from the sky, and the clouds approaching from the east were light and fluffy and would soon chase away the black and heavy ones.

He went back to bed, feeling relieved.

It was not going to be a nasty day of the kind that always put him in a bad mood.

Then he remembered the dream he'd been having when he was woken up.

He was walking through a tunnel in complete darkness except for the oil lamp in his hand, which didn't give off much light. He knew that a man was following one step behind him, someone he knew but whose name he couldn't remember. Earlier the man had said:

"I can't keep up with you; I'm losing too much blood from my wound."

And he had replied:

"We can't go any slower than this; the tunnel could collapse at any moment."

A short while later, as the man's breathing became more laboured, he'd heard a cry and the thud of a body falling to the ground. So he'd turned around and gone back. The man was lying face down on the ground, with the handle of a large kitchen knife sticking out between his shoulder blades. He was immediately certain the man was dead. At that moment a strong gust blew out his lamp and immediately the tunnel collapsed with a rumble like an earthquake.

The dream was clearly a hotchpotch resulting from an excess of *purpiteddri a strascinasale* and a news item he'd heard on television about a hundred or so miners who'd died in a mine in China.

But the man with the knife in his back, where'd he come from?

Montalbano searched his memory, then decided that it was of no importance.

Ever so gently, he drifted back to sleep.

Then the telephone rang. He looked at the clock. He'd slept for barely ten minutes.

Bad sign, if they were calling him at that hour of the morning.

He got up and answered the phone. "Hello?"

"Birtì?"

"I'm not —"

"Everything's flooded, Birtì!"

"Look, I —"

"There were a hundred rounds of fresh cheese in the storeroom, Birtì! Now they're under six and a half feet of water!"

"Listen —"

"To say nothing of the warehouse, Birtì."

"Jesus! Would you please listen to me for a second?" the inspector howled.

"So you're not —"

"No, I'm not Birtì! That's what I've been trying to tell you for the last half an hour! You've got the wrong number!"

"So, if you're not Birtino, then who is this?"

"His twin brother!"

He slammed down the receiver and went back to bed, cursing the saints. An instant later the telephone started ringing again. He jumped out of bed, roaring like a lion, grabbed the receiver, and, yelling like a madman, said:

"Fuck off, you, Birtino, and your hundred rounds of fresh cheese!"

He hung up and unplugged the phone. He now felt so upset that the only solution was to take a nice long shower. As he was on his way to the bathroom, a strange little jingle could be heard coming from somewhere in the bedroom.

And what could *that* be?

Then he realized that it was his mobile phone, which he rarely used. He answered it.

It was Fazio.

"What is it?" he asked rudely.

"Sorry, Chief, but I tried calling you on the landline, and some guy answered . . . I must have got the wrong number."

So it was Fazio he'd told to fuck off.

4

"You really must have, because I'd unplugged the phone," he lied in a confident, authoritative voice.

"Of course. Well, the reason I'm disturbing you on your mobile is there's been a murder."

How could you go wrong? "Where?"

"In the Pizzutello district."

Never heard of it. "Where's that?"

"It's too complicated to explain, Chief. I've just sent Gallo with a car for you. And I'm on my way to Pizzutello. Oh, and put on some boots. Apparently the place is kind of a bog."

"OK. See you in a bit."

He turned off the mobile phone, plugged the landline back in, and managed to make it to the bathroom when he heard the phone ring. If it was the same man looking for Birtino, he would get the address and then go and shoot the lot of them. Including the fresh cheese.

"Chief, wha', did I wake yiz?" Catarella asked apprehensively.

"No, I've been awake for a bit. What is it?"

"Chief, I wannit a tell yiz 'at Gallo's squawk car woun't start an' 'ere warn't no utter cars available inna car park o' cars for availability in so much as they was unavailable 'cuz they was unmovable."

"What is that supposed to mean?"

"'Ey're broke."

"And so?"

"An' so Fazio ordained me to come an' pick yiz up in my car."

Yikes. Catarella wasn't exactly an ace at the wheel. But there was no alternative.

"But do you know where the murder victim is?"

"Assolutely, Chief. An', jess to be sure, I'm bringin' along my talkin' naviquator."

He was downing his third cup of espresso and about to go out when he heard a sudden loud crash outside the front door. He gave such a start that he spilled coffee on his jacket and a little more on his rubber boots. Cursing, he ran to see what had happened.

When he opened the door he very nearly ran into the nose of Catarella's car.

"What are you trying to do? Break through my door and into my house?"

"Ya gotta f'give me, Chief, but 'ere was so much mud inna driveways 'at the car skidded outta control. 'Twas the mitteriolagical connishins 'at did it, not me."

"Put it in reverse and back up a little, otherwise I can't get out."

Catarella did as he said and the engine roared, but the car didn't move even a quarter of an inch.

"Chief, the driveway's onna downhill hill anna wheels can't get no traction inna bud."

"Cat, it's called 'mud', not 'bud'."

"Whate'er ya say, Chief."

"So what are we gonna do?"

"Chief, if ya come ousside tru' the veranna door and I goes in tru' the same, we can switch places."

"And what'll that do for us?"

"You'll drive and I'll push."

6

This made sense. They switched places. And after ten minutes of heave-ho, the tyres at last caught. Catarella then took it upon himself to go and lock up the house, and when he returned they changed places again and finally set off.

The talking naviquator had already been talking for half an hour, and Catarella had been obediently following its orders for that entire half hour, saying "yessir" to every direction it was giving, when Montalbano asked a question.

"But didn't we just pass the old signal box at Montelusa Bassa?"

"Yeah, Chief."

"And where's this district we're going to?"

"Still up ahead, Chief."

"But if we're already in Montelusan territory, then, if we keep going . . ."

"'Ass right, Chief, 'roun' 'ere, iss all Montelusa."

"So what the hell do we care whether somebody died on Montelusan turf? Pull over and stop. Then get me Fazio on the mobile phone and pass him to me."

Catarella did as he was told.

"Fazio, would you please explain to me why we should handle a case that's outside of our jurisdiction?"

"Whoever said that?"

"Whoever said what?"

"That it's not in our jurisdiction."

"I'm saying it! If the body was found in Montelusan territory, it's only logical that —"

"But the Pizzutello district is in our jurisdiction, Chief! It's right next to Sicudiana."

Jesus! And the two of them were on the very opposite side of town. But then there was light, inside Montalbano's head.

"Wait a second."

He glared at Catarella, who returned the stare with a slightly guarded expression.

"What district are you taking us to, Cat?"

"Rizzutello, Chief."

"Cat, can you tell the difference between a P and an R?"

"Sure, Chief."

"Then tell me what that is, when they're written in capital letters."

"Cappital litters? OK, lemme tink. So, the R's gotta belly an' a li'l leg, but the P's only gotta belly."

"Good. But you got it wrong. You're taking me to a place that's got a little leg, when you should be taking me to a place that's only got a belly."

"So I made a mistake?"

"You made a mistake."

Catarella turned first as red as a turkey and then as pale as a corpse.

"Ohhh, no! A'ss terrible, terrible, jess terrible! Unfergivable! I took the chief the wrong ways!"

Forlorn and on the verge of tears, he buried his face in his hands. The inspector, to keep things from getting any worse, patted him amicably on the back.

"Come on, Cat, don't take it so hard. A minute more, a minute less, doesn't make any difference. Chin up. And now take the phone and get Fazio to explain to you which way we should go."

To the right-hand side of a former country road, now reduced to a sort of muddy riverbed hacked up by hundreds of truck-tyre furrows, was a vast, wide-open building site that had turned into a sea of mud. Piled up to one side were a great many concrete pipes wide enough for a man to stand up in.

There was also a large crane, along with three trucks, two excavators, and three earth movers. Clustered on the other side were a number of cars, including Fazio's and the two belonging to Forensics.

Once past the building site, the road went back to being a normal country road, all uphill. Some thirty yards up you could see a sort of small house, and then another, a bit further up.

Fazio approached the inspector.

"What's the building site for?" Montalbano asked.

"They're building a new water main. The workers haven't been to work for four days because of the bad weather, but this morning two employees came here to assess the situation. It was them who found the dead body and called us."

"Have you seen it?"

"Yeah."

Montalbano noticed that Fazio was about to add something but then stopped.

"What is it?"

"You'd better have a look for yourself."

"But where is this body, anyway?"

"Inside the pipe."

Montalbano hesitated. "What pipe?"

"You can't see it from here, Chief. It's hidden by the machines. They were boring through the hillside so they could run the pipes through it. Three of them are already in place. The body was found deep inside a kind of tunnel."

"Let's go and see."

"The Forensics team are in there, Chief. You can't really fit more than two people at a time. But they're almost finished."

"Has Dr Pasquano been?"

"Yeah, he had a look and then left."

"Did he say anything?"

"The two workers found the body at six-fifteen this morning. Pasquano said he died about an hour earlier. It was clear he was shot before he went into the pipe."

"So he was taken there by whoever it was that killed him?"

Fazio looked uneasy.

"Chief, I'd rather you saw it with your own eyes."

"Is the prosecutor here yet?"

It was known to one and all that Prosecutor Tommaseo always ended up crashing his car, in every way conceivable, even on sunny days with no traffic, so one could only imagine what might happen with all the rain they'd been having. "Yes, but it's Prosecutor Jacono, because Tommaseo's got flu."

"Listen, I want to talk to the two workmen."

10

"Hey, guys! Come over here for a minute, would you?" Fazio called over to the two men, who were standing beside one of the cars, smoking.

He and the inspector slid around in the mud as they approached, then said hello.

"Good morning. I'm Inspector Montalbano. What time did you both get here today?"

The two men exchanged glances. The older man, who looked about fifty, replied.

"Six o'clock sharp."

"Did you come in the same car?"

"Yes, sir."

"And the first thing you did was go into the tunnel?"

"That was supposed to be the last thing we did, but we went in as soon as we saw the bicycle."

Montalbano paused.

"What bicycle?"

"There was a bicycle on the ground right outside the entrance to the tunnel. We thought maybe someone had gone inside to take cover, and —"

"Wait a second. How could anyone have ridden a bicycle through all this mud?"

"There's a sort of walkway, Inspector, which we made out of planks, otherwise we couldn't get around. You can only see it from up close."

"So then what did you do?"

"What were we supposed to do? We went into the tunnel with our torches and when we reached the end we saw the body."

"Did you touch it?"

"No, sir."

"How did you know he was dead?"

"When somebody's dead, you know they're dead."

"Did you know him?"

"We have no idea who he is. He was lying face down."

"Did you have any sense he might be someone who works here?"

"I don't think we could say one way or the other."

"Do you have anything else to tell me?"

"No, that's all. We came right out and I called you."

"All right, then, thanks. You can go now."

The two men said goodbye and ran away. All they wanted to do was go home. Then there was some activity around the parked cars.

"The Forensics guys have finished," said Fazio.

"Go and see if they found anything."

Fazio walked away. Montalbano would never exchange a word with the head of Forensics, not even with a gun to his head. He had a profound dislike for the man, who felt the same way about him.

Fazio returned five minutes later.

"They didn't find an empty case, but they're certain the man entered the tunnel after he was shot. There's a bloody hand-print on the inside wall of one of the pipes, as if he was bracing himself to keep from falling."

The Forensics cars drove off. That left Fazio's car and the van from the morgue.

"Here, Chief, take my arm. Otherwise you risk slipping and getting mud all over you."

Montalbano didn't turn down the offer. They walked along gingerly, taking short steps, and once they got past the two vehicles, Montalbano could finally see the hole at the base of the hill and the entrance to the tunnel.

"How long are the pipes?"

"Twenty feet each. The tunnel itself is sixty feet, and the body's at the far end."

On the ground to the left of the entrance lay a bicycle half-covered in mud, which the Forensics technicians had cordoned off with yellow ribbon attached to a few slender poles.

The inspector stopped to have a look at it. It was a rather old bike, quite worn out, and at one time must have been green.

"I wonder why he left the bike outside and didn't just ride it straight into the pipe," said Fazio. "There was plenty of room."

"I don't think he did it on purpose. He must have fallen and didn't have the strength to get back on."

"Take my torch, Chief, and go in ahead of me," said Fazio.

Montalbano took the torch, turned it on, and went in, with Fazio following behind.

After taking two steps, however, he turned and ran back out, panting.

"What happened?" Fazio asked, perplexed.

The inspector couldn't very well tell him about the dream.

"I felt short of breath. Are you sure this tunnel's safe?"

"Totally."

"OK. Let's go," he said, turning the torch back on and taking a deep breath, as though about to plunge underwater.

CHAPTER
TWO

It was hopeless. He knew it would be this way. The scene was exactly the same as in his dream, and he didn't like the situation one bit. The only difference was that Fazio, who was following behind him, luckily didn't have a kitchen knife stuck between his shoulder blades.

It was muddy inside the tunnel as well, though a lot less than outside. Still, there was plenty of mud. At last the beam of the torch centred on the corpse. Montalbano's jaw dropped.

That was because the dead man, who lay face down and looked like a statue of mud, wasn't wearing any clothes aside from a pair of pants and a sleeveless vest. He was even barefoot.

He'd been killed by a single gunshot that had hit him right between the shoulder blades. The bullet's entry wound was plainly visible in his vest, which was once white but now reddish-brown from a mix of blood and muddy water.

"I wish I could see his face," said the inspector.

"Let's go," said Fazio.

Once outside, the inspector went over to talk to the morgue orderlies tasked with transporting the body, who were playing cards inside the van.

They gave him a dirty look, kept on playing for a few minutes, then got out of the van and went into the tunnel.

"At five o'clock this morning it was raining like there was no tomorrow," said Fazio. "Why would anyone go out into the deluge for a ride on his bike, barefoot and in his underwear?"

"He wasn't out for a ride; he was fleeing," the inspector replied. "And he was probably shot after he'd already hopped on the bike. Which leads me to think . . ."

"To think what?"

"That someone mortally wounded wouldn't have the strength to cycle uphill in a storm."

"Explain."

"What's to explain? The man could only have —"

"All done!" said one of the orderlies, coming out of the tunnel.

Montalbano and Fazio went back inside. The orderlies had turned the body over and even cleaned the man's face.

The body was a good-looking young man of about thirty, with black hair and a row of healthy white teeth visible through his half-open mouth. Under his left eye he bore a scar in the shape of a crescent moon. There was no exit wound in the front of his vest, which meant that the bullet had remained inside his body.

"OK, that's enough for me," said the inspector. They went back outside.

"Can we bag him?" asked one of the orderlies.

"Be my guest," said Fazio.

Montalbano looked around. The landscape depressed him and wrung his heart. And it made him uncomfortable. The huge crane looked like the skeleton of an ancient mammoth, while the large pipes were like the bones of some gigantic, unknown beasts, and the trucks misshapen from the thick layer of mud encrusted on them were all dead. There wasn't a blade of grass to be seen anywhere. All greenery had been covered by a dark grey semi-liquid that looked in every way like open-air sewage water that had throttled all living beings from ants to lizards. Montalbano recalled a line from Eliot's "The Waste Land", the one that evokes "rats' alley/Where the dead men lost their bones."

"But how long have they been working on this water main, anyway?"

"Seven years, Chief."

"Why so long?"

"Because after five years they had to stop all work when they realized the costs had tripled. The usual stuff."

"And then they started up again afterwards?"

"That's right. They got a new subsidy from the regional administration. But in the meantime the water seems to have run out."

"What water?"

"The water that was supposed to be piped through this new main, which was supposed to come from the Voltano."

"And why does the Voltano not have any more water?"

"It's not that the Voltano doesn't have any more water; it just doesn't have enough to fill this conduit."

"Why not?"

"Well, what happened was that the Consortium of Caltanissetta won the competition for the water from the Voltano."

"So this conduit serves no purpose?"

"That's right."

"So why do they keep working on it?"

"Chief, you know as well as I do that it's because the contracts have already been granted and certain people's economic interests have to be respected or the whole affair will end up in the gutter."

But wouldn't it be better for it to end up in the gutter once and for all?

This little discussion with Fazio was exactly like the proverbial drop that makes the glass overflow.

"Let's get out of here."

"But, Chief . . ."

"No, Fazio, if we stay any longer the mud's liable to seep into my brain. I can't stand it. Go and tell Catarella to go back to town by himself. You can give me a lift home to Marinella."

He got Fazio to drop him off outside his front door. They'd agreed to meet at the station after lunch.

When he reached for the keys in the pocket he usually kept them in, they weren't there. He searched in his other pockets, to no avail. Then, cursing the saints, he realized that Catarella, after locking up the house, had never given them back to him.

He rang the doorbell in the hope that Adelina might still be inside. Nobody answered. He rang again frantically, then, to his relief, he heard his housekeeper's voice.

"Geez, whassa big hurry? Comin'!"

The door opened, and Adelina took one look at him and cried out:

"Stoppa righ' there!"

Montalbano froze, stunned. "What's wrong?"

"I jess washa da flo'! If you wanna come in here all filty witta mud, I gonna hafta star' cleanin' all over again!"

"So, in your opinion, I can't come in?"

"Tekka offa ya boots an' I bringa you somma shoes."

It wasn't easy pulling his boots off while standing in the doorway.

"I should warn you I also want to take a shower."

"Butta batroom izza spacklin' clean!"

"So I'll buff it up a little, OK?"

"I can'ta stoppa you, sir. I jess live witt it."

An hour later, after showering, changing his clothes, and leaving Adelina behind, muttering to herself as she put the bathroom back in order, he got into the car and drove off to headquarters.

He felt a lot better. The shower had washed away the mud but not the invisible muck that Fazio's words about the construction of the conduit had made him feel all the way under his skin.

The first thing he noticed as he walked in was that Catarella was not at his post at the switchboard.

"There's been no sign of him," said the officer on duty.

Want to bet he got lost on the drive back and wouldn't return until late morning?

"Would Inspectors Augello and Fazio happen to be on the premises?"

The officer gave him a strange look. Damn. The inspector had forgotten he wasn't talking to Catarella.

"Are they here?" he corrected himself.

"Yes, sir."

"Please summon them to my office."

They showed up at the same time, said hello, and sat down.

"Do you know about the guy we found murdered?" the inspector asked Augello.

"Fazio filled me in."

"Anything new at your end?"

"This morning when you guys were out, Tano Gambardella phoned."

"The journalist?"

"Right."

Gambardella ran a pugnacious weekly newspaper that dealt with all the crooked things that went on in Vigàta. He was a brave man who'd already survived two Mafia attacks on his life. He also sometimes worked for the Free Channel, whose news programme was run by Nicolò Zito, a good friend of Montalbano's.

"What did he want?"

"He wouldn't tell me."

"Why not?"

"Because he only wanted to talk to you. Poissonally in poisons, as Catarella would say."

"But you're my second-in-command! You should have —"

"Listen, Salvo, I couldn't insist because there's an old story between Gambardella and me that goes back a way."

Montalbano understood in a flash. Any "old stories" concerning Mimì could only involve one thing.

"Does it have anything to do with his wife?"

"Yes. And a fine-looking woman she is."

"And how far back does this story go?"

Mimì squirmed in his chair.

"Let's say about three months."

"Mimì, if you don't straighten yourself out, and fast, one of these days some jealous husband is going to shoot you, and I'll give him a hand fleeing justice, you can count on that. So, how did you leave things with him?"

"He'll call you back."

"OK, guys, now listen up. As I started to say to Fazio this morning, our murder victim could only have lived somewhere near the building site, and, more precisely, in the upper part of Pizzutello."

"How can you be so sure?"

"Because, mortally wounded as he was, he could never have pedalled uphill, and in the mud to boot. At best he might have been able to ride downhill, with the bike coasting on its own. And there's another important detail. He knew that there was a sort of walkway of planks above the mud which the workers had set up at the building site, but which you couldn't see with all the mud around. This means that he went that way often and had probably seen them building it."

"But why did he go into the tunnel?"

"He was trying to hide. He thought the people who'd shot him were giving pursuit."

"That doesn't make sense," said Mimì. "If he was trying to hide, he would have taken the bike inside the tunnel as well."

"He couldn't, because he fell, and I don't think he was in any condition to still think clearly. Maybe he no longer had the strength to lift the bike out of the mud."

"He must have been caught by surprise in his sleep," said Mimì.

"Exactly. Then something must have happened that allowed him enough time to hop on the bike and ride off. And then they shot him in the back, but he was strong enough to keep on riding."

"Makes sense to me," said Fazio.

The telephone rang. It was Catarella.

"Chief, I wannit a inform yiz 'at I finally manitched to retoin to da premisses."

"Did you get lost?"

"Yeah, Chief. I ennèd up in Trapani."

Montalbano hung up, feeling relieved. At least he wouldn't have to organize a search party.

"So, what do we do now?" asked Mimì.

"You stay here and fill in for me in your usual brilliant fashion. Fazio and I are going back to Pizzutello."

22

★ ★ ★

The first house past the building site, about a hundred yards away, was a sort of cross between a two-storey suburban home and a country house. Whoever built it couldn't decide whether to make a pretentious mini-villa or a proper farmhouse. To one side was a garage, which was closed. The front door faced directly onto the road. The windows were all shut.

There was no doorbell. Fazio knocked and knocked, but nobody came to the door.

After a while they abandoned their efforts and headed for the next house up the road. It was rather large and abandoned, but they could hear a chorus of hundreds of chickens behind it.

The front door was open. "May I?" asked Fazio.

"Come in, come in," said the voice of an elderly woman. They were expecting to find themselves in a perfectly normal room of a perfectly normal home, but what they entered instead was a space outfitted to serve simultaneously as a grocery shop, restaurant, and bar.

And in fact there were three small tables already laid for anyone who might want a bite to eat.

Behind the bar was an old woman with a friendly demeanour and sharp, lively eyes.

"Would you like some coffee? How 'bout some fresh eggs?"

Montalbano was dying of curiosity.

"But what kind of place is this, anyway?" he asked.

"Just what it looks like," the old woman promptly replied. "We sell bread, pasta, juice, eggs ...

everything. We can even make you somethin' to eat. An' we'll make you a good cup o' coffee, too."

"But why isn't there some kind of sign outside?" the inspector asked.

"'Cause I ain't got no licence."

"Have you ever requested one?" Fazio intervened, making a stern face.

"I wouldn't dream of it! You know how much the bribe would cost to get a licence?"

"But then this is an illegal establishment!" Fazio exclaimed.

"Establishment? You call this an establishment?" the old woman reacted, raising her voice. "At my age, I ain't established nothin' for a long time! What are you, anyway, a finance cop?"

"No, I'm just —"

"Then if you're not, don't gimme no guff!" The woman eyed them and then said to herself: "These guys are cops!"

A second later, shouting loud enough to make Montalbano's and Fazio's ears ring, she called: "Pitrineddru!"

Pitrineddru then materialized, though it was not apparent exactly how or from where.

He was a colossus of about forty, some six and a half feet tall, with a hairline practically attached to his eyebrows, biceps almost three feet in circumference, and hands the size of shovel-blades.

"Wha' is it, Ma?"

"Pitrineddru, my love, these two coppers is sayin' we's illegal, an' I'm afraid they gonna wanna shut down our store."

Pitrineddru looked at them darkly and took a deep breath, like a bull about to charge.

Out of the corner of his eye, Montalbano saw Fazio's right hand reach inside his jacket to take out his revolver. Pitrineddru turned around menacingly. It was a dangerous moment. Calmly, and in a flat voice, Montalbano said:

"Let's make a deal."

"What kinda deal?" asked the old woman, who had keen ears.

"I don't make no deals with cops!" said Pitrineddru, glowering.

"Shut up and get the hell outta here," the woman ordered him.

In the twinkling of an eye, Pitrineddru vanished into thin air.

"So, you want that coffee or not?"

"Well, all right."

"Then sit yourselves down."

Montalbano and Fazio settled down at one of the set tables. Then a man came in and asked for ten eggs, a loaf of bread, and a kilo of pasta. The old woman brought them their coffee and sat down with them.

"Let's hear about this deal."

"First you must tell me how you knew we were cops."

"Because cops — the real ones, I mean — got it written all over their faces. So, about this deal . . ."

"We won't report you to the Finance Police, but in exchange you must give us some information."

The woman's answer was immediate.

"It breaks my heart, but I never rat on no one."

"I'm not asking you to rat on anyone. I just want to ask you whether a certain person lives around here."

"Somebody wanted by the cops?"

"No, he's not wanted."

"Wha'ss his name?"

"We don't know. He's about thirty, with black hair, about five foot nine, with a crescent-shaped scar under —"

"Giugiù Nicotra," the woman interrupted him.

"Do you know where he lives?"

"I certainly do! Right here next door!"

"In the little house?"

"Yessir."

"Is he single?"

"Nossir, he's married."

"We knocked at the door but nobody answered."

"I'ss possible the slut couldn't come to the door 'cause she was too busy fucking somebody."

"Are you talking about Nicotra's wife?"

"In't that who we's talkin' about? She's a German girl, 'bout twenty-five, goes by the name of Inghi. She often comes to do her shopping here, brings her bike, all tarted up with her jeans so tight they look painted over her arse . . . When her husband ain't around, she's often 'entertainin'. An' I think she also feeds her lovers, too."

"Why do you say that?"

"'Cause whenever she comes here she buys a lot o' stuff, like there was four people in her house isstead o' just two."

"They don't have any children?"

"Nossir."

"Does he work?"

"Yessir. He's a 'countant."

"Where?"

"I dunno."

"How can you be so sure his wife entertains guests?"

"'Cause this road from Vigàta goes on to Sicudiana, an' so the cars comin' from Sicudiana have to pass by here. An' I can sometimes see someone stop at their house and then leave again about two hours later. The big slut. Just think, she even tried to do some things with my saintly boy Pitrineddru . . ."

"Listen, do you by any chance have the phone number for that house?"

"Yessir, I got it right here."

Fazio wrote it down.

"And do you know where the lady normally keeps her bicycle?"

"She just leans it up against the wall outside her front door."

"Did you hear any strange noises early this morning, around five?"

"What kind of noises?"

"A gunshot, for example?"

"Good God, it was thunnerin' like bombs this morning! I wouldna even heard a cannon go off!"

Fazio and Montalbano exchanged glances. They had no more questions.

They stood up.

"A deal's a deal!" the old woman said.

"That goes for us, too," said Montalbano.

They left, and got into the car.

"Shall we try the house again?" Fazio suggested.

"Let's."

But, once again, nobody came to the door.

"I don't know, but something about this whole thing doesn't make sense to me."

Fazio headed over towards the garage.

"Where are you going?"

"I want to see if the car's in there."

He disappeared behind the garage, then reappeared. "There's a little window for ventilation at the back. The garage is empty. Maybe the lady took the car out for a drive."

"You think it's as simple as that?"

"Why, what should I be thinking?"

"You haven't asked yourself the biggest question."

"And what would that be?"

"Where was she while her husband was being shot?"

Fazio became silent and pensive. Montalbano stood there, staring at the front of the house, which normally at that hour should have been drenched in sunlight. But there was no sun that day; it was covered by heavy black clouds. Montalbano went behind the house. Fazio followed him. Back there, it already seemed like night.

CHAPTER
THREE

Looking up, Montalbano noticed immediately that there was some light filtering out through the slats of a shuttered window on the upper floor, Fazio also saw it.

"By architectural logic, that should be a bedroom," said the inspector.

"That light has probably been on since last night," Fazio added.

Montalbano then had an idea and went round to the front of the house again.

"Let's try one last time," he said to Fazio. "Take your mobile phone and dial the number the old lady gave you."

The inspector went up to the door and put his ear against it. Everything around was perfectly silent.

However hard he tried, he couldn't hear a phone ringing inside. Was it possible there was no phone on the ground floor? Or perhaps someone had cut the cable?

"Are you calling?"

"Of course."

"How come I can't hear a phone ringing?"

"Let me try," said Fazio, taking the inspector's place. He listened for a few moments and then said: "It's ringing. Far away, but it's ringing."

"So how come I couldn't hear it?"

Fazio looked at him but thought it best not to answer. And Montalbano immediately regretted asking.

There was no doubt about it. Not only, with the years, did he not see so well, but he was also going a little deaf. *Matre santa!* Going around with glasses as thick as Coke-bottle bottoms he could perhaps tolerate, but a hearing aid was absolutely out of the question. At that point he might as well retire to an old people's home, as Pasquano was always advising him, just to annoy him.

"I must have too much wax in my ears."

"Of course," Fazio said, looking up to follow a bat flying wildly overhead.

Were those two words the only thing he knew how to say?

"Let's go back to the office," Montalbano said brusquely.

"What do you think you'll do?" Fazio asked as he started the car, realizing that the inspector had fallen into a bad mood and that it was best to try to distract him.

"It's too late now, but tomorrow morning I'm going to see Prosecutor Jacono and get authorization to enter that house."

"Think you'll get it?"

"Jacono usually doesn't make any fuss."

"What do you expect to find there?"

"Well, if you really must know, I've got a bad feeling. I think we're going to find a dead woman in there."

"I'm afraid you're probably right," said Fazio. "But what do you think happened?"

"I don't like to play guessing games."

"Just to pass the time . . .?"

"There are a number of possible hypotheses. One thing is certain, however, and that's the starting point: Giugiù Nicotra, and maybe his wife, were surprised in their sleep. And I'm convinced it wasn't by burglars."

"What makes you say that?"

"A burglar doesn't shoot his victim in the back as he's running away. Whatever happened, the intruders make them get up out of bed just as they are and go downstairs."

"Why do you say that?"

"Because if they'd remained upstairs Nicotra would never have had a chance to run outside. He wouldn't have even had time to go downstairs."

"You're right."

"Once downstairs, they start looking for something, or at least they want something the couple has."

"How do you know that?"

"Fazio, if someone breaks into somebody's home at night and it's not a burglar, there are only four possibilities. It's either one of the wife's lovers, or a kidnapper, or someone looking for something, or someone who wants to know something. But I would rule out the first two cases."

"Go on."

"As the intruders keep questioning them, Nicotra sees an opening. Maybe a moment of inattention on their part. He opens the door, knowing that his wife's bike is always there outside, leaning against the wall. He hops on it and rides off. One of the two men shoots at him and hits him between the shoulder blades. But Nicotra is able to sustain it and keep pedalling into the night. Bear in mind that there's a storm as all this is going on. And so, since they can't do anything else, they kill the woman and leave."

"I'm sorry, but why did they take the car? Which we can assume they did, since it's not in the garage."

"I really don't know. Maybe they didn't actually kill the woman but only kidnapped her."

"So how should we proceed?"

"Tomorrow morning, when I'm off to see the prosecutor, I want you to find out as much as you can about Giugiù Nicotra."

"Should I say we've identified the corpse?"

"It's probably better to wait on that. We'll make it known after I've talked to the prosecutor."

"OK, you can praise me now," said Mimì Augello, face beaming as if on a grand occasion as soon as the inspector walked in.

"What heroic feat have you accomplished?"

"In the space of two hours, I've carried out the sort of thing the newspapers call 'a brilliant operation'."

"Tell me about it."

"As soon as you and Fazio left I got an anonymous phone call. An unknown man told me that a certain

Saverio Piscopo, residing at Via Lo Duca 4, had received a big shipment and hidden it in his three-month-old son's pushchair. He added that he was reporting this to the police because Piscopo was dealing outside schools."

"And you trusted an anonymous phone call?"

"Yes, and I was right. There was a kilo of grass in the pushchair, together with a lot of chemical stuff."

"Did you arrest him?"

"Of course."

"How did he react?"

"The guy's a good actor, you know. He pretended he knew nothing, and he couldn't explain how the stuff had got into the pushchair. He kept on repeating that he made an honest living as a bricklayer. So, are you gonna praise me or not?"

"Well done, Mimì."

He stood up and was about to go out of his office and home to Marinella when the phone rang.

"Chief, I gotta tell yiz, 'ere's a soitan Mr Gambabella onna line."

He would have bet the family jewels that Gambabella was actually Gambardella.

"Hello, Gambardella, what can I do for you? I know that you already —"

"Yes, Inspector, and I apologize for any trouble I may be causing you. But this concerns something very serious, and I rather urgently need to talk to you in private."

"Well, I was just on my way out, but I could stay a little longer and —"

"I apologize again, but I don't want anyone to see me going into your police station."

So this wasn't something to be taken lightly. If they were keeping an eye on him . . .

"I see. Do you know where I live?"

"Yes."

"It's eight o'clock. In half an hour, say?"

"OK."

The first thing he did when he walked into his house was check to see what Adelina had made him for dinner. Opening the oven or fridge at such moments gave him the same feeling he used to get as a little boy, when he used to break an Easter egg to see what was inside.

Perhaps to make up for her gruffness that morning, Adelina had cooked him a glorious *pasta 'ncasciata* and two big links of sausage in tomato sauce.

What with the nasty weather, fresh fish were hard to come by. There was frozen fish galore, but they weren't fit for his palate.

He would warm it all up after Gambardella's visit.

He opened the French windows onto the veranda, but sitting outside was out of the question.

The doorbell rang, and Montalbano went to greet his visitor. It was Gambardella.

Reading his fiery articles and knowing the kind of risks he ran, one might imagine Gambardella as a cocky bull of a man with a defiant gaze, whereas in fact he was a tiny bloke of forty-five with a bald head and spectacles who wore a jacket whose sleeves were too short.

They sat down in the two armchairs in front of the television, but turned them to face each other.

"Something to drink?"

"No, thanks. I don't want to take up any more of your time than is strictly necessary."

"Well, I'm going to have a little whisky."

"Do you read my newspaper?"

"Yes. Among other things, I think calling it *The Lighthouse Guardian* was right on the money."

"Thanks. As I'm sure you know, I'm a lawyer by trade, with a passion for journalism. And as a journalist I have this nasty habit of looking for skeletons in people's cupboards."

"In these corrupt times, I wouldn't call that a nasty habit but a real virtue."

"Though a virtue that — as many have made me fully understand — might cost me dearly. But I'll get to the point. Have you ever heard mention of a company called Albachiara?"

"No."

"It was founded a year and a half ago for the purpose of building public works. About a month after it was set up, it went on the market — a market already teeming with hardened competitors, mind you. Be that as it may, Albachiara, among other things, won the contract for a school complex in Villaseta. They finished the work in record time and fourteen months later turned over the keys to the complex."

"How much did they inflate the costs?"

"Very little. A negligible percentage. In that respect, they behaved unimpeachably."

"So, a perfectly respectable firm, in other words."

"In appearance."

"Meaning?"

"A month ago, exactly one week after their inauguration, one of the three buildings was declared unfit for use."

"Why?"

"Two ceilings had collapsed and some rather obvious damage appeared in the outer walls."

"Was anyone injured?"

"Luckily, no."

"Did they open an investigation?"

"They had no choice but to."

"And what was their conclusion?"

"They found that the construction company was not to blame. The damage to the walls was caused by a landslide beneath the building."

"I'm sorry, but isn't it required procedure, before beginning any construction, to check the risk factors in the ground?"

"Of course, and it was done."

"And everything was in order?"

"Yes. The authorization was signed by Professor Augusto Maraventano, an expert in such matters, though by then he was already ninety years old and senile."

"I get it."

"It gets even more complicated."

"Was Maraventano ever called in for questioning?"

"That wasn't possible."

"Why?"

"He died six months ago. And that's where the story ends: everyone kissed and made up. Nobody was found guilty."

"But, you see —"

"Wait. Having come this far, I asked myself an entirely logical question."

"What?"

"If the ground is unstable, aren't the other two buildings also at risk?"

"And what did you do?"

"I went to speak to Professor Maraventano's assistant, an engineer by the name of Riccio, who assured me that the story about the landslip was a lie that Albachiara and the judge had agreed upon. The ground apparently was extremely solid, from a geological point of view. He showed me the surveys, the studies and analyses, everything. The problem was that nobody — other than me — took the trouble to go and talk to him."

"But how could the judge have —"

"He only consulted the survey report drawn up by someone suggested by Albachiara. And so I arrived at the inescapable conclusion."

"And what was that?"

"That the material used by Albachiara was not what was stated in their contract, but something vastly inferior in quality. And, furthermore, that they saved a lot of money in the construction itself, by skirting specific rules concerning stability and safety. I started moving in this direction three days ago, asking around for people's opinions."

"And?"

Gambardella smiled.

"And yesterday in my letterbox I found an envelope with the address written in block capitals. That immediately aroused my suspicion, and so I opened it. All it contained was a photo of my son, Ettore, who is six years old, as he was coming out of school."

"No message?"

"Nothing."

"Do you have the photo with you?"

Gambardella reached into his coat pocket, took out an envelope, and handed it to the inspector. It hadn't been postmarked, so someone must have slipped it into the letterbox. The photo showed a little boy laughing as he spoke to a friend who was out of the picture but for his shoulder. "Worth a thousand words," said Montalbano as he handed him back the envelope. "And what do you intend to do now?"

"Starting tomorrow, Ettore will go to school in Montelusa and live at my sister's house."

"You think your son will be out of danger in Montelusa?"

"I'm not that stupid. But at the moment, I can't think of . . ."

"Go ahead and send him to Montelusa for the moment, but don't let him go to school. Take him to your sister's place this very evening, and make sure nobody knows about it."

38

"All right."

"So you intend to proceed with your investigation?"

"I think that's pretty clear."

"I want you to know that I'm entirely at your disposal in this affair. You need only tell me how I can —"

"I just came here to inform you of the threat I'd received. If anything should happen to me or someone in my family, you'll know where to start your investigation."

"I'll make you an offer."

"I'm listening."

"I can't take any action, in an official capacity. But if you keep me informed of everything you find out as you go along, it'll make it easier for me to prevent any dangerous moves on their part."

"All right, then."

"One final question. Who have you spoken to?"

"Three former bricklayers who'd worked on the construction of the schools. One of them, a certain Saverio Piscopo, gave me a tip that might prove valuable."

"What did you say his name was?"

"Saverio Piscopo."

Who'd already paid dearly for having talked. They'd put drugs in his boy's pushchair. He chose not to give Gambardella this news.

"What was the tip?"

"That initially the site foreman for the school complex was Filippo Asciolla, who was then sacked and replaced. I was told that Asciolla is hopping mad at the

Albachiara people. I want to go and talk to him as soon as possible."

"Keep me posted on that, and be very careful. Oh, and listen, do you know the name of the company that is constructing the new water main for the Voltano, and whose current building site is in the Pizzutello district?"

"Where a man was found murdered this morning?"

"Yes."

"The company's called Rosaspina."

"What are people saying about this murder?"

"Since the man hasn't been identified yet, there's endless conjecture, and naturally some people suspect some seamy sex story behind it all. For now, though, it's all just talk."

As soon as Gambardella left, Montalbano laid the table while the food warmed up in the oven. Then he relaxed and savoured it all slowly, especially the *pasta 'ncasciata*.

Once he'd cleared the table, he turned on the TV and watched the news on the Free Channel.

Since he had quite purposely not yet told anyone the dead man's name, he was referred to simply as "the anonymous victim". Nicolò Zito, the newsreader, expressed surprise that no one had filed a missing persons report so far. Because — and here he came to the same conclusion as the inspector — a man who goes out in the pouring rain at five in the morning in his underpants and hops on a bicycle can only live somewhere nearby. And he concluded.

"With no information forthcoming yet from the police, we shall begin our own investigation tomorrow morning, and we shall keep our viewers up to date as it proceeds."

Smart guy, Nicolò, you had to admit. But then something occurred to the inspector.

Nicolò surely wouldn't take long to work out that the victim lived in a house near the building site and was married. And by making this news public, he would put the killers on their guard, effectively helping them to defend themselves. This had to be avoided. But how? The best way would be to fill Zito in and find out exactly how things stood. But that meant he had no time to waste waiting for the prosecutor's authorization. He had to get moving on his own.

The telephone rang. At that hour it could only be Livia. He didn't feel like getting up and answering. Then he made up his mind, but before picking up the receiver he had another moment of hesitation.

He picked it up.

"How are you feeling?"

For the past three days Livia had had a fever and a touch of the flu.

Before that, she'd had stomach problems, and before that, she'd had such pains in her legs that she couldn't walk . . .

The truth of the matter was that ever since the death of François, she was no longer the same. She'd changed a lot.

She seemed to have lost all interest, forgot things, neglected her appearance, was no longer present even to herself.

Now, just hearing how different her voice sounded, Montalbano felt his heart give a tug. The world around him turned grey and a wave of melancholy swept over him.

"A little better," she said. A pause, and then:

"I wish you were here."

"I promise I'll come. As soon as I can."

"I feel so alone . . ."

She no longer had the strength to go to work. She'd taken a leave of absence from her job and hadn't wanted to come down to Sicily because she thought she would just be a weight around his neck. And now she just stayed holed up at home all day.

The words came out of his mouth by themselves. "Livia, please, I beg you," he said. "Try to react, do it for us, for both of us. You're everything to me. When I hear you sound like that, I . . ."

"I'll try, Salvo, I promise. Good night."

"Good night."

He put down the receiver, took a deep breath, and ran a hand over his face. It was wet.

CHAPTER
FOUR

Seen by the light of the full beams, on an utterly moonless night with the sky entirely covered by a heavy blanket of clouds blacker than the blackest night, the building site looked like the perfect set for a German Expressionist film, with the sharp contrast of lights and darks and the gigantic, deformed shadows looking like projections of monstrous, motionless figures.

Or one of those other pictures, usually American, about the day after a nuclear catastrophe, when the survivors wander about a landscape they knew perfectly well the day before but now do not recognize, so foreign has it become. It was as though nobody had worked at that building site for many years: the crane, the trucks, the excavators looked just like skeletal scrap metal abandoned centuries earlier on some dead planet.

All colour was gone. One saw nothing that wasn't the same drab, uniform grey as the mud. Or the "bud", as Catarella called it. And maybe he wasn't wrong to do so, because the mud had entered the blood, become an integral part of it. The mud of corruption, of payoffs, of phoney reimbursements, of tax evasion, scams, faked balance sheets, secret slush funds, tax havens, *bunga bunga* . . .

Maybe, thought Montalbano, it was all a symbol of the situation in which the whole country found itself at that moment.

He stepped on the accelerator, in the sudden, irrational fear that the car might get infected, come to a stop at that accursed place, and turn into another muddy ruin between one moment and the next.

Had this happened, he would surely have started screaming at once like a frightened child, and it would have taken a long time before he regained the use of his reason.

He heaved a sigh of relief when his headlights at last lit up the front of the house.

But they also lit up a car that was parked a bit to one side.

Want to bet someone had had the same idea as him? But could Zito the journalist have possibly already got so far in his private investigation?

It took him a moment to realize he couldn't stop, that he had to pretend to be just driving by, and so he kept on going. He did, however, manage to notice distinctly that there was a man and a woman inside the car. They were both sitting in the front, and when his full beams shone on them they moved so that their faces would not be seen. She was blonde.

It couldn't be Zito.

He passed the old lady's illegal shop and drove on until the country road joined the main road to

Sicudiana. There was almost no traffic at that hour. He pulled over to the side and stayed in the car.

He lit a cigarette and smoked it slowly. Good thing there was almost a whole pack, since, in one way or another, he had at least half an hour to kill.

Because of the couple in the car, what he had in mind to do had now become a bit more dangerous than expected. For there was a chance — a small one, of course, but a chance — that the blonde woman was Inge, Nicotra's German wife, who was returning home completely unaware that her husband had been murdered and wanted to say, well, one last goodbye to the man accompanying her.

The half-hour, by God's grace, finally passed. Montalbano started the car and retraced his path.

The car with the couple was gone. Had it actually been an amorous tryst, or had Inge gone straight inside after saying goodbye?

He got out of the car and stood motionless for a spell, to check whether any headlights were approaching. On so dark a night one would see the beams from miles away. Luckily there was nothing. Pitch-black in both directions.

He walked cautiously towards the house.

There was no light filtering through the shutters at the front. He went round the back. The situation seemed the same as that afternoon. Except that the bedroom light was more visible.

He came back round the front, tiptoeing ever so softly, to avoid making any noise, and opened the door on his third try, using a special key he'd been given by an old burglar. Pushing the door gently, and slowly, worried that it might creak, he craned his neck and looked inside.

The darkness on the ground floor was so dense, so solid, that you could cut it with a knife. Before entering, he took off his shoes, leaving them outside.

Going in, he turned on the powerful torch he'd brought and closed the door behind him, guiding it gently with his hand.

His immediate impression was that there was no one in the house. It smelled stuffy, of stale air.

This meant that the woman in the car was not Inge. The coast was clear, but proceeding carefully, in such situations, was the golden rule.

The torch beam revealed that he was in a large room divided into an alcove kitchen in one corner, an eating area, and a third part fitted out as a sitting room. At one end was a closed door, no doubt a bathroom.

He'd imagined a different scene. Here, instead, everything was in perfect order. The only things that looked out of place were an overturned chair in the middle of the room and another lying on its side.

A clear sign there'd been something of a scuffle, the beginnings of a struggle.

Then he noticed some muddy footprints left by a pair of shoes and a pair of heavy boots, leading from the door and going straight to the foot of the wooden staircase.

So two people had come into the house.

He moved slowly towards the stairs, then started climbing them, trying not to make the slightest sound.

46

The staircase led to a corridor with three doors in a row on each side.

The first room at the top of the stairs was a bedroom. As the light was on, it corresponded with the one he'd seen from the outside.

He went in.

The sheets and blankets on the double bed were thrown over to one side and touched the floor.

A pillow covered in blood had fallen on the floor.

It seemed immediately clear to Montalbano that only one person had slept there.

How to explain the blood? Whose was it?

The murdered man's head, which he'd seen with his own eyes, showed no wounds.

He continued his inspection. The next room was a spacious bathroom, followed by a sort of study. He went over to the other three rooms facing the front of the house. Directly across from the study was a storeroom, then came a bathroom just like the other one, and finally a bedroom with a double bed.

Here, too, the bed was in a state of chaos, and it was clear that two people had slept in it.

This left Montalbano bewildered. So Nicotra and his wife had a guest. Male? Female?

Then he had an idea, and opened the wardrobe. There were men's as well as women's clothes, the latter a little gaudy. That must therefore have been the master bedroom. He had his confirmation when he went into the bathroom next to it. There were perfumes, creams, make-up.

He went back into the first room and opened the wardrobe. Three men's suits, grey and blue, two woollen sweaters . . . all belonging to a man of a certain age. And shirts, underpants, socks . . .

He took the suits out, one at a time, thoroughly searching the pockets. No papers, no documents.

He closed the wardrobe and went and had a look in the bathroom. Razor blades, shaving brush and soap . . .

He'd forgotten to inspect the little drawer in the bedside table. Going back into the bedroom, he opened the drawer and the first thing he saw was a large revolver, loaded, and, beside it, a box of cartridges. There was nothing else. But on the bedside table, next to a bottle of water, was a phial of medicine with a dropper attached to its cap. It contained heart medication.

So the man must not have been someone passing through, but a sort of permanent guest.

He couldn't have been a relative, otherwise the old woman would have mentioned him.

Indeed, the old woman must not even have been aware of him, since she was surprised to find that they spent too much on food for just two people.

So who was he? And what was he doing in that house? And had the intruders taken Inge away because she was a potentially dangerous witness?

In conclusion, the situation had, in a sense, worsened: now there was one murder victim and two people kidnapped.

There was nothing more to be done in the house. He went back downstairs, turned off his torch, and opened the door. But to see where he'd left his shoes, he had to turn the torch back on.

And that was how he managed to notice a metallic glint somewhere very near his shoes. He felt around until he found what it was. An empty case. One hundred per cent certainly from the gun that had fired the shot into Nicotra.

And this proved, in part, the inspector's reconstruction. He left the case where he'd found it, put on his shoes, closed and locked the door, got into his car, and drove off.

As he was driving to Marinella he started thinking about some things that didn't add up.

The first was the story the old woman had told him, that is, that Inge received visitors, because cars would sometimes pull up outside the house and then leave a few hours later.

How could Inge have been fucking her occasional lovers so brazenly, not giving a shit about the old man staying at her house? This would have meant that he, among other things, had to have been her accomplice, not to have revealed anything to the cuckolded husband. No, this seemed inconceivable.

And so it was legitimate to make another, more reasonable hypothesis. The men who parked their cars outside the house were not going there to meet Inge, but the person staying there. And it was convenient for

Inge to let people think she was a slut, so that nobody would suspect that a man was hiding in their house.

The other thing that didn't add up was the elderly guest himself. Why was he staying there? What was his relationship with the owner of the house? Why were people coming to see him?

And, most importantly, why, when he slept at night, did he keep a revolver within reach?

The inspector was unable to answer even one of these questions.

But this did not prevent him, when he finally got into bed, from having an excellent sleep.

The following morning, before going to Prosecutor Jacono's office, he dropped in at Montelusa Central Police to talk to Angelo Micheletto, the new chief of Narcotics, who was a good friend of his and with whom, between jokes and banter, he had exchanged many favours.

"Listen, 'Ngilì, I've got a sensitive matter on my hands I want to talk to you about confidentially, like a brother," said Montalbano, putting on a serious face.

"Well, I'm the most sensitive person you know, little brother. Confide away," said Micheletto, making the same face.

"Following an anonymous phone call yesterday, my second-in-command, Mimì Augello, unbeknownst to me, arrested some poor bastard for possession of drugs, a certain Saverio Piscopo, who —"

"Save your breath, I know all about it. What do you need from me, brother?"

"You need to know that Piscopo is not a dealer; he was set up, in retaliation."

"And how do you know that?"

"Piscopo's an informer of mine," said the inspector, making as sincere a face as possible.

"Ah, I see. And your second-in-command was not aware of this?"

"No."

"I questioned Piscopo myself. Can you explain to me why he didn't tell me he was an informer of yours?"

"I have no explanation."

"Well, I do. It's because he's not an informer of yours, and you just made that up to get him out of trouble."

At this point, the only solution was to lay his cards on the table.

"You're right."

"No, no, no! Brothers don't lie to each other! At any rate, just to set your little heart at rest, you should know that I, too, became convinced that Piscopo was not involved in any way in drug-trafficking. We turned his life inside out like a sock, and found that all he'd ever done was work as a bricklayer. He's clean."

"So you're setting him free?"

"This very morning. But I mean it: next time, don't come to me talking crap."

To the prosecutor he told the whole story, except, of course, for the part about the nocturnal visit.

"So you think it's absolutely necessary to get into that house?"

"I see no other way to move forward on the case. If you have a better idea —"

Jacono had no better idea. "When would you go?"

"First thing this afternoon."

"Let me know immediately if you find the woman's body in there," he said firmly as he signed the authorization.

He'd made the inspector wait two hours to see him, but he'd wasted no time making up his mind.

The moment Montalbano entered the station he told Catarella to ask Fazio and Augello to meet him in his office. Then he said to Fazio:

"Can you go outside for a minute? I need to speak to Inspector Augello in private."

Fazio got up and went out. Augello gave him a questioning look.

"Mimì, I'm going to have to retract the praise you extorted from me over your brilliant arrest of Saverio Piscopo. He turns out to have no connection whatsoever with drug-trafficking."

"But we found drugs in the —"

"I know, but somebody planted them there on the sly and then called you so that he would be arrested."

"Who told you this?"

"The chief of Narcotics, that's who. Good enough for you? So, next time, think carefully before believing an anonymous phone call."

Furious, Augello got up and went out without saying a word. A moment later, Fazio came in.

"I got Jacono's authorization," said Montalbano. "Tell Forensics to be on the scene by four o'clock. They're the ones who must unlock the door. If we find Inge dead inside, we'll have to alert the prosecutor and Pasquano. And what have you got to tell me?"

"Can I read the notes I jotted down on a piece of paper?"

"On the condition that you don't, as usual, start with the subject's great-grandparents."

"OK. Gerlando Nicotra was born thirty-four years ago in Vigàta and got a degree in accounting. He was the son of an accountant."

"Are his parents alive?"

"The father, yes, and I've got his address and telephone number. But not his mother."

"Go on."

"He's been married for five years to Inge Schneider, born in Bonn, twenty-nine years old. We know where they live. He seems to have been a pretty serious young man, hard-working, no vices, no women on the side. Clean record. He'd recently bought himself a new car, a Volvo. I've got the licence-plate number, which might prove useful. For the last year and a half he was the chief accountant for Rosaspina."

"What does that mean exactly, 'chief accountant'?"

"It means he handled payouts and salaries, reviewed expenditures for materials, and balanced the books as well."

"A position of responsibility, in other words."

"Absolutely. He knew about practically every cent that came in or went out."

"One second, Fazio. But isn't Rosaspina the one building the water main?"

"That's right. But Nicotra wasn't always at the site; he worked in an office."

"Therefore it's likely the two workers didn't recognize him."

"Yes, they probably didn't."

"And before working for Rosaspina, what did he do?"

"He was an accountant for Primavera."

What poetic names these firms had! Firms which, to get the public works contracts, were capable of the vilest things.

"But that's a little strange," Fazio continued.

"Why?"

"If you recall, I already told you that before Rosaspina got into the act, the company working on the water main came under investigation for fraud, and there were arrests and convictions and they eventually lost their contract. That company was in fact Primavera."

"So what's strange about that?"

"The only former employee of Primavera hired by Rosaspina was Nicotra."

"Are you sure they didn't take on anyone else?"

"Absolutely certain."

"Not even any of the workers?"

"Not even."

"Maybe he's a good accountant."

"Good accountants are ten a penny."

"Then there can only be one explanation: he's got friends in high places."

"That's possible. In fact people say that in order to hire Nicotra, Rosaspina had to sack the accountant they'd just hired."

"Anybody whispering who recommended him?"

"One rumour has it that someone on the board of directors — Nino Barbera, a lawyer — wanted him."

"Anybody know why?"

"For the simple reason that, based on what people say, he was sleeping with Nicotra's wife."

"So it's the usual story."

"Apparently."

"You're not convinced."

"No."

"Tell me why."

"I know this lawyer Barbera. He might well have been Inge's lover, but I know that he's small potatoes on the board of directors. There must be another reason. I just can't work out what."

"Maybe Nicotra's name was pushed on Barbera by one of the other directors he couldn't say no to. But we're still in the realm of conjecture. And you know what you have to do to take us from conjectures to certainties."

"Yeah, I know."

Montalbano started to feel irked. "Then if you know, tell me."

"Find out the names of the board directors."

"Bravo. Now get up, inform yourself, and report back to me."

"Already taken care of," said Fazio, taking another piece of paper out of his pocket.

Montalbano saw red. Whenever Fazio said that, he lost control. To let off steam, he pinched himself painfully on the thigh with his right hand, which was out of view.

"Can I read it?"

"Go ahead, go ahead."

"Michele La Rosa, engineer, chairman of the board; Giovanni Filipepi, medical doctor; Nicolò Transatta, landowner; Mario Insegna, businessman; and Nino Barbera, lawyer."

"I don't know them. Do you?"

"I know two of them. Barbera the lawyer and Dr Filipepi. It's well known that he's the Cuffaro family doctor."

As if the Mafia wouldn't be involved in this affair! They were always up to their necks in the shady business of public contracts.

"Are the Cuffaros his only patients?"

"No, Chief. He's a good doctor, and he's got a lot of patients. You can see them queueing up outside his office."

"Then the fact that he also cares for a Mafia family might not mean anything."

"Or it might mean many things," Fazio felt compelled to add with a pensive air.

"If you have any suspicions, all you have to do is get moving," said Montalbano.

"That's what I've been wanting to do."

CHAPTER
FIVE

"Meanwhile," said the inspector, "as we're sitting here talking, something is happening that doesn't make sense to me."

Fazio gave him a befuddled look.

"As we're sitting here talking?" he asked.

"Exactly."

"What is it?"

"First answer a few questions for me."

"Go ahead."

"Did Rosaspina, like every other company in the world, have an office with an office manager?"

"Sure. It's on Via —"

"Never mind the address, I'm not interested in that, at least for now. What's the office manager's name?"

"Wait a second while I look."

He dug the piece of paper out of his pocket, ran his eyes over it, and then said: "Pasquale Ranno. He's a surveyor."

"And what time is it right now?"

Fazio, completely bewildered, took a look at his watch and said: "Twelve minutes past twelve."

"Excellent. Finding himself shot and killed, yesterday, chief accountant Gerlando Nicotra was prevented from going to the office by circumstances beyond his control and wasn't in a position to explain his absence. Correct?"

"Correct."

"So my question is: how is it that, by early afternoon, no one has got in touch with us yet? Not a single phone call concerning the accountant's disappearance?"

"You're right," said Fazio. "But there may be an explanation. Maybe they called the carabinieri."

"Could you find out?"

Fazio left and returned five minutes later. "There haven't been any reports."

"This is starting to smell fishy to me. It's as though they knew immediately who the murder victim was. And if that's the way it is, they made a huge mistake. A mistake of omission. They should at least have pretended to be upset."

"Think it's possible the workers who discovered the body did recognize it, even though they said nothing to us?"

"The body was face down and covered in mud. No, if they did know who it was, that wasn't how they found out."

Catarella appeared in the doorway.

"Chief, ascusin' the distoibance for cummin' 'ere in poisson, but the tiliphone at the moment momentarily don't woik. I wannit a tell yiz 'at Nicotra the 'countant's 'ere onna premisses."

But wasn't he dead? Montalbano and Fazio exchanged a confused look.

"Are you sure that's his name?"

"Swear onna Byber, Chief."

Fazio slapped his forehead. "It must be his father!"

"Show him in," said the inspector. Then, turning to Fazio:

"What did I tell you about not hearing anything from Rosaspina? How much do you want to bet that his father is here because he has no news of his son?"

"I don't like to lose bets."

"Hello, my name is Ignazio Nicotra," said a slender, well-dressed man of about seventy with an aquiline nose, a halo of white hair, and thick glasses, as he came in.

He had a worried look on his face and felt quite uncomfortable, as could be seen from the slight tremor in his hands and his Adam's apple, which kept bobbing up and down.

"Please sit down and tell us what we can do for you."

"I may be a bit apprehensive by nature, and I'm probably just wasting your time, but the fact is that I'm worried about my son Gerlando."

"Why?"

"Because, since he doesn't live with me, and I'm a widower, he normally phones me twice a day, early in the morning before going to work, and again in the evening when he goes home. Yesterday he didn't call me, and he didn't call this morning, either."

"Did you try to get in touch with him?"

"Of course. I spoke to his office manager, Mr Ranno, who told me that they didn't have any explanation for Gerlando's absence, either. Also because Gerlando always makes sure to let them know when he's running late or not coming in to work."

"When was the last time you saw your son?"

"Six months ago."

"But do you live in Vigàta?"

"Yes."

"So why so long without . . ."

Ignazio Nicotra squirmed in his chair, threw up his hands, and shook his head a few times.

"I used to go to their house every Sunday for lunch. Then, about six months ago, Gerlando told me it would be better if I stopped coming round, at least for a little while. He'd been quarrelling with Inge, his wife. Apparently she liked to go out for lunch on Sundays, and my presence . . ."

He trailed off. Montalbano made a mental note that the unknown visitor must have been in that house for six months, and that was the real reason they kept the father away.

"I'm going to have to think for a moment about what steps we should take," said Montalbano, who meanwhile was racking his brains trying to think of how to give him the bad news.

But it was the old man himself who put him on the right track. After clearing his throat, Mr Nicotra said:

"Just last night I heard that a man was found dead at the Rosaspina building site — that's the firm my son works for — and hasn't been identified yet. And so I had a terrifying thought, and I didn't sleep all night. Could I see the body?"

"Yes," Montalbano said immediately. "But first —"

He stopped himself and looked over at Fazio, who nodded his approval.

"Excuse me for a moment," he said to the old man.

And he got up, ran out of the room, went down to the car park, and lit a cigarette.

Fazio would take care of preparing the man little by little. Montalbano would never have had the nerve.

Some twenty minutes later he saw Fazio come out, supporting the poor father, who didn't have the strength to stand on his two feet. Fazio sat him down in his car, and then came over to the inspector.

"I'm driving him to Montelusa for the official identification. I'll see you back here at three."

Every once in a while he didn't feel like eating.

He was picturing the scene of the old accountant in front of his son's lifeless body in the livid light of the morgue, and his stomach twisted into a knot as tight as a fist.

He'd read somewhere that in France a great artist from the Abruzzi had been hired to make a morgue less gloomy and sad. What a great idea!

He decided to go home. As soon as he got back, he slowly sipped half a glass of whisky, then went out onto the beach.

At the water's edge, the stormy seas of the past few days had deposited a long, broad strip of rubbish on the sand. Plastic bags and bottles, containers of every sort, bottomless shoes, old tyres, tins, jerry cans, all of it covered by a nasty sort of grey foam that not only looked like mud but had a strong, bad smell. It stank of rot, of decaying, dead matter . . .

Once upon a time — but when? a thousand years ago — the tides used to wash up seaweed, starfish, and shells on the shore . . . And what a wonderful smell they had! Essence of sea water . . .

There was a time when Livia used to collect seashells. They once even quarrelled over it.

"You know something strange, Salvo? The ones I find in Boccadasse are more beautiful."

"Of course."

"Since you concur, can you explain why?"

"Because the ones in Boccadasse are fake, made of plastic."

"What are you saying?"

"I know it from a reliable source. The employees of Pro Loco scatter them on the beach for the tourists."

Livia didn't get the joke and flew into a rage. Livia! Oh, God!

A wave of emotion as unexpected as it was unstoppable swept over him, forcing him to run back inside, grab the phone, and dial her number.

It rang a long time with no answer. Not expecting any calls at that hour, Livia had unplugged the phone. Perhaps to get a little rest. So much the better.

He took a shower, made a cup of coffee, dawdled about the house for a while, and then went back to the office.

Fazio was already there and told him that after the heart-rending identification, he'd taken the old man, who'd seemed more dead than alive, back home and left him in the care of some neighbours. And so, what with one thing and another, he hadn't had time to eat.

They decided to take a squad car with Gallo at the wheel and go back to the victim's house.

As they were driving there, Fazio asked:

"What do you make of the answer Ranno the office manager gave to Gerlando's father?"

"You mean that they had no explanation for his absence, either?"

"Yeah."

"It's an answer that unwittingly puts the icing on the cake of my suspicions about the way they're acting. What? You have no explanation and you do nothing to find out? It can mean only one thing: that you do have a hypothetical explanation, but you prefer to sit tight and wait to see how the situation develops."

"I see it the same way. And what about the fact that Gerlando hadn't wanted his father to set foot in his house for the past six months?"

For his part, Montalbano did have an explanation for this, and a rather clear one, but he couldn't tell Fazio.

"I don't know what to say to you. Maybe the story about Inge not liking him is true."

Though it wasn't raining, and in fact a hint of wan and decidedly short-lived sun had appeared, nobody was working at the building site. Apparently Jacono still had it under a sequestration order.

It wasn't yet three-thirty when they pulled up in front of Nicotra's house. Gallo had sped the whole way. The Forensics team hadn't arrived yet. They got out of the car.

With an air of indifference, Montalbano went up to the front door. He wanted to check whether the cartridge case was still there. It was. He wanted to play it safe.

"Fazio!"

"What is it, Chief?"

"Come over here beside me and look at where I'm pointing. Do you see it? Is it what I think it is?"

"Yes, it is. It's a cartridge case."

"We have to make sure that the Forensics guys don't trample it into the ground when they walk around here."

Fazio picked up four large stones and put them around the case to protect it.

Forensics arrived ten minutes later. Luckily the chief of the department hadn't come. In his place was his assistant, Jannaccone, an intelligent man Montalbano liked a lot.

Fazio showed him the case. It was photographed and then put in a plastic bag.

"Shall we unlock this door?" asked Jannaccone.

"Let's," said the inspector.

As an officer was fiddling with the door, Jannaccone asked:

"What do you think we'll find inside?"

"This was the home of the man who was found dead from a gunshot wound inside the tunnel. I hope I'm wrong, but I'm afraid we're going to find the corpse of a woman, his wife, inside."

He told this lie with the aplomb of a great actor, face serious and dark.

"They didn't have any kids?"

"No. Just the two of them lived here."

He said this on purpose. He wanted the presence of a third person to be a surprise for Jannaccone, too, to get his attention and arouse his curiosity.

"We'll go in first, and then I'll call you," said Jannaccone.

"Success," said the officer at the door.

Some ten minutes later, with Montalbano already on his third cigarette, Jannaccone came out again.

"We didn't find any bodies."

"So much the better," said Montalbano, sighing with fake relief.

"But there weren't two people living here, as you said, Inspector. There was a third person as well."

Montalbano looked at Fazio with a masterly expression of surprise. Fazio's, however, was authentic.

"A third person?"

"That's right."

"Listen, Jannaccone, I absolutely have to —"

"I'm sorry, but I can't let you go in. There are muddy footprints on the floor which —"

"Please."

It was a word of entreaty, but uttered in a tone of command that permitted no refusal. Jannaccone got the message. He shook his head, then shrugged in resignation.

"Well, all right. Come in behind me in single file and don't touch anything for any reason."

They went in. The lights had been turned on. Fazio looked around as if to photograph everything.

"There was a struggle here," he whispered behind Montalbano, seeing the two chairs on the floor.

"Right."

The scene was already etched in the inspector's brain.

Jannaccone took them upstairs and into the room across from the staircase.

"This was the room the other person was staying in. His hosts slept in the one in front."

"But that pillow is bloodstained! They must have beaten him!" said Montalbano, feigning surprise.

"They probably punched him in the face to make him get up and get dressed," said Jannaccone.

"Could you open the wardrobe for me?" the inspector asked.

Jannaccone opened it.

"The guest was a man and, to judge from the colour and the cut of the suits, probably wasn't young. You can close it now, thanks."

When they went back out into the hallway, Fazio ventured to ask:

"Could we see the other bedroom?"

"OK, but still in single file, please."

As soon as they entered, Fazio made an observation, more to himself than to the others.

"Why did they take the clothes?"

"What clothes?" asked Jannaccone, who hadn't understood.

Montalbano explained.

"Clearly both the woman and the third person were made to get dressed before they were kidnapped. But the murder victim's clothes are also missing, even though he'd managed to hop on a bicycle and escape in time and was found wearing only a vest and pants. All that's left here are his shoes."

"Wait a minute," said Jannaccone.

He went out and returned almost immediately. "They're not in the bathroom, either."

"It's clear that his clothes were taken by the assailants," the inspector concluded. Then, heaving a sigh, he continued:

"Listen, Jannaccone, we absolutely have to find the identity of the person sleeping in the other room."

"Look, Inspector, we have the blood on the pillow and we're certain to find a whole lot of fingerprints. It'll take a while, but we'll manage."

"How long?"

"I expect there won't be enough time today and we'll have to continue into tomorrow morning. But since, luckily, there's no corpse here, we can work completely undisturbed."

"Then I don't think there's any point in us staying here."

"No, I don't think so, either."

On the drive back, neither Montalbano nor Fazio said a word.

Each was reflecting in his own way on what he had seen in the house.

They talked about it as soon as they got back to the station. "Who," asked Fazio, "do you think was the old man staying with the Nicotras?"

"I don't know and I don't want to make any pointless speculations. Let's wait and see what Forensics can tell us. All I can say for certain is how long he'd been there: six months."

"How do you know that?"

"Gerlando's father himself told us, indirectly, when he revealed that his son hadn't let him set foot in the house for the past six months."

"That's true. And they kept him well hidden, to the point that neither the old lady up the road nor Gerlando's father even mentioned him. But what about the missing clothes?"

"They must have taken them to avoid wasting time looking for his mobile phone, wallet, the papers he had in his pocket . . . They didn't know whether or not they'd hit Gerlando, and so they might have been worried he would send for help . . ."

"But now I'm wondering whether we're really looking at the whole affair from the right perspective," said Fazio.

"Meaning?"

"I'm wondering whether the guys that came in were after Gerlando or the old man."

"There's only one thing I'm starting to be sure of. If Gerlando hadn't run away, there wouldn't have been any murder, only three kidnappings. And if all had gone according to plan, it would have lasted only a day or two, and nobody would have been any the wiser."

"But Gerlando and his wife weren't rich enough to pay a ransom."

"Maybe not Gerlando or his wife, but what do we know about the old man? Anyway, a ransom doesn't always involve money."

There was a pause.

"What are you thinking?" asked Montalbano.

"I'm racking my brains trying to figure out what that man could have been doing in the Nicotras' house. At first I'd thought they were maybe keeping him prisoner . . ."

"Come on! There weren't any ropes or gags in his room."

"Right. I could see that he was being treated like a sort of boarder. You got any ideas about that?"

"In my opinion, he'd been entrusted to Nicotras' care. Somebody must have assigned them the task of looking after him."

"Maybe he's a fugitive?"

"It's possible. But Nicotra's house doesn't seem like the best place to hide someone wanted by the law. The old lady — just to cite one example — told us that there were often cars going there. You don't go and pay a visit to a fugitive in broad daylight and out in the open."

"Maybe his visitors were friends and relatives . . ."

"That's also possible. But there's still a question that hasn't been answered. If he wasn't a fugitive, why was

69

he hiding? What were his reasons? Whatever the case, they must have been very serious, because when someone found out where he was staying, they burst in and kidnapped him, and they didn't hesitate to shoot to kill, either."

"So he must be a big cheese," Fazio concluded.

Montalbano looked at him pensively.

"That may just be the right word for it," he said.

CHAPTER
SIX

The inspector devoted his last half-hour at the office to signing the papers he'd been told were the most pressing. He'd once tried a little experiment. He'd taken a memo at the top of which were the words *Extremely urgent: reply at once*, and he'd put it in a drawer. Months and months went by, without anyone noticing he'd never replied. And so, convinced as he was that it was all a pointless bureaucratic ritual, nowadays he always signed his name wherever he was supposed to, without ever reading as much as one line of what was written in the document. And the method worked to perfection, to the point that he'd never received any criticism about it from the administration.

At last, deciding he'd worked enough and earned his day's pay, he got up and went out of his office. Walking past Catarella's desk, he noticed he was busy trying to solve a crossword puzzle. His brow was furrowed and he was chewing the end of his pencil.

"Need any help?"

"Yeah, Chief. I can't tink of a woid."

"What's the definition?"

" 'Together with the carabinieri, they pursue killers and thieves and maintain law and order.' "

"How many letters?"

"Six."

"Police."

"Are ya sure? I tought o' that, but then I arased it."

"Why?"

"When have us police ever woiked t'getter with the carabinieri?"

Iron-clad logic.

"Well, then I guess I'm wrong. Have a good evening."

He got in his car and headed home to Marinella.

The minute he was out on the road, he felt suddenly, overwhelmingly hungry, like a crazed dog that hadn't eaten for days. He hadn't felt like having any lunch, and now his body was clamouring for reinforcements without further delay. Then, twenty yards before the turn that led to his house, he had to stop because there was a line of cars in front of him with no end in sight.

What could have happened? At that hour there normally was some traffic, of course, but not so much as to create that kind of jam. Probably an accident caused by some drunkard or addict at the wheel, as seemed to be happening more and more often.

The unexpected stop so aggravated his hunger that he couldn't see.

He began to curse all the saints he knew the names of, with every possible variation of theme.

Finally, to top things off, he realized he was out of cigarettes.

At that point he couldn't take it any more and, biting his tongue, began the perilous manoeuvre of trying to

72

pull out of the queue and drive against the oncoming traffic.

At that exact moment he heard a siren approaching. It was a carabinieri squad car. He let it pass and then tagged along behind it. He covered the twenty yards in a flash and made the turn to his house.

After unlocking the front door, he dashed into the kitchen, drooling.

Adelina had prepared him a double serving of *sartù* and — finally! — a generous helping of fried calamari and shrimps. The latter, after such long privation, he savoured slowly, every so often moaning with pleasure.

After clearing the table, he went into the bathroom and washed his face over and over with cold water. It was a kind of preparation before phoning Livia. Having done this, he felt more relaxed and therefore better able to handle the heartache that Livia's sad, faraway voice was sure to cause him.

He dialled her number.

The days of the long night-time phone conversations that often ended in a squabble were over. Livia nowadays went to bed early, dead tired from having to get through yet another day.

From the start he noticed her voice had changed. It sounded much more lively, and this cheered him up.

"Feeling better?"

"A little. Today was a beautiful day and I took advantage of it to go out and buy some necessities."

"Well, you should go out in any case, every day, get some fresh air, a little exercise, walk around . . ."

Was he mistaken or did Livia give a little giggle? If only it was true!

"I think that starting today I'll be forced to do just that."

Montalbano felt confused.

"Forced by what?"

"Guess."

"I can't."

"A little creature that at this moment is sleeping in my lap."

The inspector understood immediately. "You got a dog?"

"I had no choice. This tiny little puppy started following me on the street and wouldn't leave me alone. It touched my heart, and so I took it home."

"You were perfectly right to do so. It'll be a true companion. But you should have it looked at by a vet."

"I plan to go tomorrow morning."

Good! That way, what with one thing and another, and having to take the little dog out for walks, she'll get back into the habit of going outside every day.

"What'll you call it?"

"I haven't decided yet."

They talked for a little while longer, then said good night and sent each other a long-distance kiss.

In his mind Montalbano lit a very large candle and put it at the foot of the statue of the unknown saint — there had to be one — who protected animals.

Then he sat down in front of the television to watch the ten o'clock news. Tuning in to TeleVigàta, he was curious to hear what they had to say about the Nicotra murder.

TeleVigàta was very often more than happy to serve as an unofficial spokesman for the Mafia. It was well known that the station's shareholders included front men for both the Cuffaro and Sinagra families.

Pippo Ragonese, their top newsman who always found ways to attack Montalbano and speak ill of him for one thing or another and discredit him in the eyes of the Vigatese, appeared on screen.

. . . late this morning we learned the identity of the victim's father. We were able to get in touch with Inspector Domenico Augello of the Vigàta police, but he told us he was not at liberty to release any information. This is Montalbano's style, consisting almost entirely of unjustified haughtiness and utter scorn for the need for information. Unfortunately it is the rule with the Vigàta police. Among the various theories circulating as to the motive for the murder, there is one that stands out as the most convincing, one which we feel it is our journalistic duty to bring to our viewers' attention. The beautiful young Inge, wife of the late *ragioniere* Gerlando Nicotra, was, according to the vox populi, inclined, one may say, to partake in extramarital adventures. On that fateful night, Nicotra, who was in the habit of taking pills that would plunge him into a deep sleep, unexpectedly woke up to find that his wife was not lying beside him. When, after a while, she didn't come back to bed, he got up and, hearing some whispering downstairs, cautiously went and looked down from the top of the stairs. And he saw his wife in another man's arms. Arming himself with a pistol, he went downstairs and threatened the pair. His wife's lover, not the least bit intimidated, managed after a brief struggle to disarm Nicotra, who, fearing for his life, tried to flee on his wife's bicycle. The lover then shot at him and immediately fled in turn with Signora Inge. This is merely a hypothetical reconstruction, but it is, we repeat, the one we find the most convincing. It is, moreover, well known that *ragioniere* Nicotra was a man of impeccable conduct and a model employee who . . .

He turned it off, having found out as much as he needed to know.

As far as he could remember, and on the basis of everything he'd read, the tradition in Sicily was that every Mafia crime, right from the start, must be made to look like the consequence of adultery.

The following day brought the gift of a triumphant sun in a cloudless sky.

Montalbano was so pleasantly surprised that he started singing, off-key as usual, "*E lucean le stelle . . .*"

Even after his shower he carried on his bel canto display, but it came to a sudden halt when he thought he heard the telephone ring.

He pricked up his ears, right hand in the air, holding the razor.

Nothing.

Maybe it had rung for a bit and then stopped. And so?

And so, dear Salvo, you may just happen to be going deaf.

His good mood suddenly evaporated and was replaced by a surge of anger at himself.

"I can hear perfectly well! Got that, idiot?" he said to the face reflected in the mirror.

And the face in the mirror replied:

"Idiot? Look who's talking! You're the idiot for not wanting to accept reality!"

"What reality?"

"The reality of your age!"

The spat was cut short by the ringing of the phone.

"See! I can hear just fine!" the inspector yelled into the mirror before going to answer it.

It was Mimì Augello.

This fact took him aback. Augello normally never called him at home, and Montalbano would rather it have been someone else bothering him.

"Was it you who called a few minutes ago?"

"Yes."

Damn! So the phone really had been ringing.

"What is it, Mimì?"

"I want some instructions."

"On what?"

"On whether I should believe what I learned from an anonymous telephone call I just received."

It all became suddenly clear. The stupid bastard Augello was getting even for the scolding he'd given him. But Montalbano had no choice but to play along.

"What did you learn?"

"That a car was torched last night in the Riggio district and it's still smoking."

"OK. Go and see what's up with that."

"Are you sure?"

Mimì's ironic tone put him on his guard.

"About what?"

"About whether I should go?"

"Why not?"

"Because Fazio, who's standing here beside me, tells me that Riggio district is right next to Pizzutello."

"Damn!" Montalbano exclaimed.

"See? . . . Be seein' ya. Here's Fazio."

"Hello, Chief? I'd say it's worth our while —"

"To go and have a look? I agree."

"I'll come with Gallo's car to pick you up in half an hour, max."

Driving past the deserted building site, they saw the two Forensics cars parked in front of Nicotra's house.

"Shall we ask them how far along they are?"

"No, let's keep going."

The old woman's illegal bar-restaurant was open and hopping. One customer was on his way out, carrying a small plastic bag, while another was coming in.

About a hundred yards farther on there was an unmade road on the right. Gallo turned onto it, and immediately the car transformed into a boat on choppy seas. The road was an endless sequence of mounds and pits the car had trouble climbing out of.

The landscape, too, had changed.

All around, as far as the eye could see, the land looked as if it hadn't been farmed for many years, becoming an expanse of weeds interrupted every so often by the ruins of some old peasant's house that now, white as they were, looked like bones in the desert.

But had there really once been lemon groves here? And orange groves? Or had it all just been a poetic fantasy?

Not to see any people or dogs about was almost normal. What was sort of chilling and made one uneasy was that there weren't even any birds in the sky.

Nobody in the squad car said a word; the desolation made one clam up.

"But are we sure this cursed anonymous phone call wasn't just a practical joke?" Montalbano asked at one point, feeling fed up.

"There it is," said Fazio.

To their left, the sloping ground was covered with thousands of white stones that seemed to have been purposely put there to form a sort of circumscribed space, and right in the middle of it, like some kind of funerary monument, lay the burnt shell of the car.

Gallo turned off the road and pulled the car up close. They all got out.

The acrid odour of melted paint, rubber, and vinyl seats was still strong.

Both the boot and the bonnet lid were half-raised and crumpled.

They were relieved to discover at once that there was no body inside.

Fazio read what remained of the rear licence plate.

"There's no doubt about it," he said. "This is Nicotra's car."

Montalbano remained silent.

At that moment a green snake almost five feet long came out from between two white stones, swiftly grazed the inspector's shoes, and took cover under another stone.

"At least there are a few living creatures around here," said Montalbano.

"I'm wondering what this all means," said Fazio. "If Inge's body was in the car, then it would make some sense and we could work a few things out, but this way . . ."

"It's clear that we weren't summoned to this godforsaken place by someone who'd just happened to see a torched car here. Whoever called us was one of the people who torched it. He wanted us to know. And that explains why they remained anonymous."

"But why did they do it?"

"To use us as postmen."

"I don't understand."

"We're required to report officially that we found this car, right? That way, whoever's supposed to get the message will get it. Apparently there's some kind of negotiation going on."

"I still don't get why they dragged this car out here."

"They had no choice."

"Could you explain?"

"The two guys who went into Nicotra's house had only one task: seize the old man. They would lay him down on the back seat, covered by a blanket, and take him wherever they took him. The Nicotras they would leave alive, but in no condition to sound the alarm, at least not immediately. The only problem was that Gerlando thought it best to run away, and so one of the two men shot him. At this point everything changes. The two men no longer know what to do, and so they weigh their options and decide to kidnap the woman as well. So one of them takes the old man into his car, putting him in the back, and for this reason the other is forced to take the Nicotras' car in order to make off with Inge. Make sense to you?"

"Yeah. So, what do we do now?"

"Now we go back to the station. The sooner the better. This isn't the kind of place we want to hang around any longer than we need to."

"Shall I alert Forensics?"

"Of course. Even though they won't find anything. But that's what they want us to do, and so we, like the good little boys we are, will give them some rope."

"I'll tell them when we drive past the house. There's no point calling them on the phone."

As he entered, he said to Catarella: "Get me Augello."

"'E ain't onna premisses, Chief."

"What do you mean he's not on the premises?"

81

"Ya mean ya donno what 'at means? You kiddin' me, Chief? It means he ain't on 'ese 'ere premisses but on some utter premisses."

Montalbano pretended he hadn't heard.

"What? So when I'm not here, and Fazio's away with me, he just goes his merry way? Who's going to hold the fort?"

"I am, Chief," Catarella said proudly.

Montalbano decided not to comment.

"But did he leave word where he was going?"

"Nah, Chief."

"How long has he been away?"

"Less say a li'l over two hours, Chief. Right after Fazio went out to get yiz at home, Isspecter Augello got a phone call and ran out rilly fastlike an' took Sargint Vadalà wit' 'im."

"Call his mobile for me, would you?"

"Straightaways, Chief."

Moments later:

"Iss toined off, Chief."

One of these days I'm going to turn him off! the inspector thought. He didn't say it because Catarella was right in front of him, looking as though he felt guilty for the fact that Augello couldn't be reached.

Montalbano went into his office in a rage. What kind of way of doing things was this? Did Augello possibly not realize the sort of catastrophe that could occur if the only person running the station was Catarella? Say, for example, the commissioner decided to pay a surprise visit . . . The idea made him shudder. The moment Augello got back, he would eat him alive.

Fazio appeared.

"Chief, I just got a call from Vadalà, who went out with Augello because —"

"Ah, good, tell me why. So I can finally know what the hell is going on in my police station!" Montalbano exploded.

Fazio, who didn't know the reason for the inspector's anger, continued by force of inertia.

". . . because somebody shot Saverio Piscopo."

"And who's he?"

"What do you mean, 'who's he'? Don't you remember? He's the bricklayer Augello had arrested . . ."

Montalbano remembered and broke out in a cold sweat.

Not only because of the news, but also because he was starting to lose his memory as well. If that was the case, it was time for the old people's home.

He wouldn't even be good at walking Livia's dog, because he would end up losing the way. Deaf, blind, and scatterbrained. Not self-sufficient. Even the retirement home might not want him.

"What?" he said, noticing that Fazio was telling him something. A second later, fearing that Fazio might see this as confirmation that he was losing his hearing, he added:

"Sorry, I was distracted."

"I was saying that luckily they didn't kill him."

"They didn't?"

"No, but he's in a serious condition. He was taken to Montelusa Hospital. Vadalà says they're finishing their questioning of the witnesses and will be back in about half an hour."

Once Fazio went out, he thought it would be a good idea to call Gambardella, but found his phone turned off.

They were making Piscopo pay for the fact that he'd talked to a journalist, first by trying to send him to gaol with a false accusation, and then by trying to kill him.

It was a clear, precise warning: whoever collaborates with Gambardella is risking his life.

It was therefore obvious to everyone and his dog what the situation was. Everyone was free to talk to the journalist, or not to talk to him.

A clear sign that the journalist had stuck his finger into a hornets' nest.

CHAPTER
SEVEN

Augello got back about twenty minutes later, his face as dark as a storm cloud. He was visibly angry and in a state over what had happened.

"Catarella told me you got upset because . . . I'm sorry, Salvo, but when I heard it involved Piscopo I was taken by surprise, since I'd been the one who —"

"You're forgiven several times over, Mimì. Now take a seat, calm yourself down, and tell me what happened."

"The poor bastard had just gone out to look for a job when a motorcycle with two men on it came up behind him and one of them shot him in the nape of the neck, hitting him squarely."

"A professional."

"Absolutely. Piscopo fell to the ground. The motorcycle stopped and the gunman, who was sitting behind the driver, got off the bike to give him the coup de grâce. But he didn't manage because a sergeant from the Finance Police fired two shots at him. So the man got back on the motorbike and drove off without firing back. Somebody called an ambulance, which luckily came at once."

"Did you go to the hospital?"

"Yes."

"What sort of condition is he in?"

"Very serious. They still have to extract the bullet, which apparently only grazed his brain. But he should make it."

He paused and looked at the inspector.

"Are we sure this isn't some settling of accounts between drug dealers?"

"Mimì, they tried to kill him for something that has nothing whatsoever to do with drugs. Did any of the witnesses recognize either of the men on the motorbike?"

"They were wearing full helmets." Another pause. Then:

"Salvo, just to set my mind at rest: would you please tell me what this is about?"

Montalbano brought him up to speed on the investigation Gambardella was conducting.

"If things are the way you say they are, I'm starting to get a little scared," said Mimì.

"What do you mean?"

"I mean those guys are liable to finish the job they started, right there in the hospital. I'm sure of it. They've failed twice, so they'll be more dogged than ever."

"You're right. There's one thing you can do. Call Prosecutor Jacono and ask him for authorization to have one of our men posted on guard duty, night and day, outside Piscopo's room."

"I'll go there right now and talk to him directly," said Mimì. "See you later."

The moment the inspector set foot in the trattoria he was overwhelmed by a great din of voices and laughter. All the tables in the room, including the one he sat at daily, were taken, mostly by youngsters all wearing the same blue and white jersey. He stopped in his tracks, bewildered. Enzo came up.

"I moved you into the small room next door."

"But who are they?"

"They're the Vigàta football team."

Montalbano didn't understand a thing about football. The small room next door had only room for two tables, and both were empty. So much the better. He would eat in peace. He ordered some antipasti. While he waited, a young man in his mid-twenties, wearing the blue and white jersey, appeared in the doorway.

"I beg your pardon, Inspector."

"Come on in."

The youngster entered. He seemed intimidated, and remained standing.

"What is it?" the inspector asked.

"My name is Nicola Piscopo, I'm Saverio's nephew. If you could do me a favour . . ."

"Concerning what?"

"This morning I asked at Montelusa Hospital if I could spend the night with my uncle and they said no. I thought that if you could maybe put in a good word for me . . ."

"I don't have the authority. But at any rate, your uncle is in good care at the hospital."

"I don't have any doubt about the care. I'm worried about other things."

They exchanged a glance and understood each other. "Well, if it'll make you less concerned, I've requested authorization to post an armed guard outside your uncle's room."

"Thank you," said the young man. He gave a half-bow and left.

Jannaccone showed up at the Vigàta police station first thing that afternoon.

"Since we'd finished and were passing through on our way back to Montelusa, I thought . . ."

He wasn't required to report to Montalbano, but was doing him a courtesy.

The inspector thanked him and summoned Fazio.

"It took us all this time," Jannaccone began, "because we kept stubbornly looking for something that absolutely had to be there but which we were unable to find. Only at the end did we have our explanation."

"I'm sorry, Jannaccone," said Montalbano, who hadn't understood a word. "What were you unable to find?"

"The old man's fingerprints."

It was as if he'd fired a gun. Montalbano's and Fazio's jaws dropped.

"It seems to make no sense, but it's true," Jannaccone continued. "I'll give you just one example. The man kept a small phial of heart medicine on his bedside table. Well, there were no fingerprints on it, not even on the glass he kept beside it."

"Do you think the assailants wiped them away?"

"I was immediately convinced it wasn't them. It would have been practically impossible to erase all the fingerprints of a man who'd been living for months in the same house, and to do so in such a hurry. And to erase the fingerprints of only that man, mind you, leaving those of the Nicotras all over the place."

"And so?"

"Well, we solved the mystery almost by chance, when I had the idea to go and search through their bin. We found two pairs of very dirty cotton gloves. Apparently the old man wore them at all times and never took them off, for any reason, not even when he went to bed and fell asleep."

"Did you find any gloves for later use?"

"No. Possibly the stock ran out and they were about to buy a new supply, maybe that same day."

"Which means," Montalbano observed, "that if that man was so concerned about leaving fingerprints, it must be because they're on file."

"I was thinking the same thing," said Jannaccone. "And I want to tell you about another strange thing. In the drawer of the old man's bedside table we found a 9mm Russian-manufactured revolver."

"Which confirms that the man was no angel."

"But the best part," Jannaccone continued, "is that another, identical revolver was found in the drawer of Nicotra's bedside table."

"Russian guns?" inquired the inspector, wanting further confirmation.

"Yes."

"They may have come through the same conduits as all the Kalashnikovs," Fazio concluded.

"As if they were standard-issue weapons, in short," said Montalbano.

"Exactly," Jannaccone agreed.

"Especially since I don't recall Nicotra having a licence to own a weapon."

"As for the others, we've got a tremendous amount of fingerprints. It'll be a long, tedious job trying to compare and contrast them. We'll see if we're any luckier with the blood that was on the pillow."

"One last question. The cartridge case that was recovered outside the front door, what make was it, do you know?"

Jannaccone smiled.

"No, Inspector, they shot Nicotra with the most Italian of Berettas. The love of our country is safe."

"What do you make of it?" asked Fazio.

"The most obvious thing: that the people who put the old man in the Nicotras' custody were worried about the possibility of an attack and so armed them both. But they didn't give them time to react. So the question goes back to being what it always was: who was the old man? With the follow-up question being: and why was he such a high-value target?"

"And how do we find the answer?"

"By trying, first of all, to put our thoughts in order. By tomorrow morning, I want you to tell me the first and last names and ages of all the Mafia fugitives in the province."

"But you yourself said he couldn't be a fugitive."

"That was just conjecture. Of which I'm still convinced, moreover. But now we need confirmation."

"Am I interrupting?" Augello asked from the doorway.

"No, Mimì, come in. What did the prosecutor tell you?"

"The idiot kept me three hours in the waiting room this morning and then didn't call me in."

"That's a nasty little habit of Jacono's."

"Later, in the afternoon, he finally deigned to grant me half an hour, but there was no persuading him to put an officer on guard for Piscopo at the hospital."

"Why not?"

"Because the bastard just dug in his heels, that's why. But, speaking of the hospital, I dropped in there while I was in town. The operation was a success, and Piscopo's going to recover. I heard this from a doctor who was speaking to the newspapermen and TV journalists."

"So they'll try to kill him again. And they'll try as soon as possible, to catch us by surprise. Maybe even tonight, which would make the biggest impression and shut up anyone who might be thinking about talking."

"I think you can bank on that."

He'd said something to Piscopo's nephew that was rather like a promise. He now had to keep it.

"OK, then, here's what we'll do. You choose first. Either from eleven to two, or from two to five."

"I don't understand."

"The two of us are going to stand guard for Piscopo. We're not authorized to do so, but nobody can prevent us. Anyway, since we're volunteers, they won't have to pay us overtime."

"What about me?" asked Fazio.

"We'll need you for tomorrow night."

"I'll take the first watch," said Mimì.

"Then find out what ward he's —"

"I already know everything. Intensive care. Second floor, on the left. He's in a single room, number eighteen."

He went home early, ate only the aubergine parmigiana to keep things light, quickly said good night to Livia, who seemed rather uplifted by the puppy's company, and then went to bed.

He got three good hours of sleep, and the alarm clock used up all its juice before he could open his eyes.

He washed himself hastily, didn't shave, and to make up for it drank two cups of espresso and headed off to Montelusa. There was nobody on the road.

At five minutes to two he pulled up in the nearly deserted hospital car park, took his pistol out of the glove compartment, put it in his jacket pocket, got out of the car, and went into the hospital.

"Where are you going?"

In the lobby was a nightwatchman sitting behind a desk with four telephones and other gadgets.

"I'm Inspector Montalbano."

"Ah, yes. Your colleague told us you'd be coming. You can go on upstairs."

Naturally, as always happened to him in hospitals, he got into the wrong lift. In the end, he gave up and took the stairs. The hallway was illuminated with the sort of night-light that seems to make more darkness than light. The door to room eighteen was closed. He knocked lightly.

"Who is it?"

"Montalbano."

The door opened, and Augello appeared. "Come on in."

The room was divided into two parts by a glass wall with a door in it.

On the other side, which was more spacious, lay the man who must have been Piscopo, with his face bandaged and a great many wires leading from his body and into some mysterious machines that buzzed like flies.

On this side of the glass there was barely enough room for a small table and two chairs. Mimì had set them up so that he could sit in one and put his feet up on the other.

"How'd it go?"

"A total bore."

"So much the better."

They said goodbye and Augello left.

The first thing that occurred to the inspector was that he hadn't brought anything to read. Big mistake.

Three hours spent doing nothing would take a whole lifetime to pass.

The second thing was that if he sat there for even as little as an hour watching Piscopo, who was rigged up so that he looked like something out of an American hospital movie, he would go insane and start bashing his head against the wall.

He did note, however, that it would have been impossible for anyone to come through the main entrance without being stopped by the nightwatchman. Maybe it would be easier trying to enter through A&E.

Still, to stay holed up in that space the way Mimì did was out of the question. Sitting there bottled up with the target of a possible assassination meant having little room to move.

And so he took the chair, put it out in the hall, went out of the room, closed the door, and sat down.

After a while his eyelids started to droop. *Matre santa!* He was falling asleep!

He heard some footsteps approaching and sat up in his chair. It was a nurse on her way to a nearby room, which she entered, staying inside for some ten minutes. Then she came out again, walked away down the corridor, and silently disappeared.

A sudden, overwhelming desire to smoke a cigarette came over him. Three rooms down to the right, at the end of the hallway, were some French windows. If he could manage to open them, he could smoke outside and comfortably keep an eye on room eighteen.

He got up, went over to the French windows, and turned the knob. It opened.

He then manoeuvred so that he had enough room to keep his body half inside and half outside.

As he was reaching for his pack of cigarettes he noticed that the little terrace outside served as a landing for a fire escape.

He stopped and thought about this.

Good thing he'd got the urge to smoke! Because the fire escape, which was something that hadn't occurred to him, would have been the best way for someone to enter the hospital without being seen.

But neither did he want to be seen from outside, even if there was little chance of this, given the pitch-darkness.

He went and got the chair and put it in front of the French windows. He could sit in it without being seen from outside.

He could finally light his cigarette.

He'd almost finished it when he distinctly heard, in the total silence of the night, a metallic sound coming from the iron staircase. It lasted a second, then vanished.

What could it have been?

Then he realized. It was the sound made when someone pulled out the bottom part of the staircase, to bring it down to the ground.

His hearing was fine, excellent! No problem there! So someone was coming up the stairs.

What should he do now? Go outside and arrest him at once, or wait for him to come up to the French windows?

He chose the second course of action.

Ever so softly he closed the door, pulled the chair away, cocked his revolver, and flattened himself against the wall in the wan glow of a distant night-light.

He waited.

Then a man appeared outside on the little terrace, and slowly, carefully, opened the French windows.

He barely had time to take a step into the hallway before Montalbano appeared before him, gun in hand.

"Police! Stop right where you are!"

For a fraction of a second, the man froze.

Then he reacted, silently and lightning-fast, landing a solid punch in Montalbano's face. The blow was so hard that the inspector staggered backwards a few steps as the blood began to flow out of his crushed nose.

Meanwhile the man had gone back out onto the terrace and was racing down the fire escape.

Still dazed, the inspector also ran outside and yelled: "Stop or I'll shoot!"

But the man ignored the warning and continued rushing down the stairs, skipping two steps at a time.

Montalbano began to do the same.

The man reached the bottom and started running towards the car park.

Montalbano also reached the bottom, and at that moment an accomplice he hadn't spotted dealt him a powerful blow to the back of the head with the butt of his pistol.

Montalbano fell to the ground, cut down like a calf at the slaughterhouse.

He didn't know how long he lay there unconscious.

When he came to, he had a terrible headache. His shirt and jacket were covered with blood, which must have come from his head.

There was absolute silence all around. Nobody'd witnessed what had just happened.

Managing to stand up, he staggered towards A&E.

It was by the grace of God.

He calmed down a little when no fracture was found. He got off lightly, with three stitches in the back of his head.

"*Matre santa! Madunnuzza beddra!* Wha' happen, Chief? Didja get inna car crash? Wit' all doo rispeck, ya gotta nose 'at looks like a aubergine! 'Dja hoit it?"

"Yeah, it was a crash, but nothing serious. Send Augello and Fazio to my office and then get me Prosecutor Jacono on the phone."

Fazio and Augello came in and gasped.

"What on earth happened?" asked Mimì.

"What happened is that you're one lucky bastard."

"What have I got to do with it?"

"If you'd taken the second watch on guard *you* would now be the one with a nose like an aubergine and three stitches in the back of your head."

"What are you saying? It was pure chance!" Augello protested.

The phone rang. It was Jacono. Montalbano turned on the speakerphone.

"I wanted to speak to you, sir, to inform you that last night an individual broke into Montelusa Hospital to try to assassinate Piscopo."

Jacono must have been taken aback by this, because there was a moment of silence before he spoke.

"What are you talking about? Who told you that?"

"Nobody told me. It was me who chased the man away."

"But what were you doing at the hospital?"

"I was guarding Piscopo's room. And before I got there, my second-in-command, Mimì Augello, had done the same. You know, he's the one who came to you to ask for protection for Piscopo. Which you obstinately refused. If we hadn't been there, you would now have to answer for a very serious mistake."

"Well, I didn't think —"

"And now you've changed your mind?"

"Well, I guess circumstances —"

"Then let me give you some advice. Have Piscopo transferred to another hospital, and keep the news of the transfer secret. If you leave him where he is, they will try again, whether we post a guard or not. Have a good day."

He hung up, relieved.

"Now tell us how it happened," said Mimì.

Montalbano told them everything.

"But when the man came in, was he carrying a weapon?" asked Fazio.

"No, he wasn't. He couldn't very well walk down the hallway openly carrying a gun. If a doctor or a nurse suddenly came out of a room . . . But you can be sure he was armed, as was his accomplice at the bottom of the fire escape."

"But why didn't you fire at him as you were chasing him down the stairs?" Augello asked.

"Because I realized they had no intention of shooting at me or making any kind of noise. Their assignment was to quietly liquidate Piscopo and finish the job they'd started."

CHAPTER
EIGHT

Montalbano then turned to Fazio and opened his mouth, but his right-hand man didn't give him the time to utter so much as a syllable.

"Already taken care of," said Fazio.

The blood rushed to Montalbano's head and he saw red. Whenever Fazio said those four accursed words, he could barely control himself. This time, however, the dam broke.

"What the bloody hell!" he exploded, slamming his fist down on the desk.

Fazio and Augello first looked at each other in shock and then turned their questioning faces to the inspector.

Montalbano realized he had to give some kind of an explanation, but of course not the real one. As often happened in these situations, however, nothing came to mind.

He started stammering.

"I . . . just suddenly remembered . . . I suddenly forgot that . . . Just never mind, OK? It's a private matter . . . I apologize. Let's carry on. What was I saying?"

"You were asking me if I'd made a list —"

"— of the Mafia fugitives, yes, now I remember. So you did?"

"I did," Fazio replied.

And he pulled a small sheet of paper out of his jacket pocket. Before beginning to read it, however, he wanted to reassure the inspector, who was already giving him a dirty look.

"No personal particulars other than first and last names and age," he said.

"Wait a second," Augello cut in. "Care to fill me in on what you two are talking about?"

The inspector explained everything in fine detail, after which Fazio was finally able to read his piece of paper.

It turned out that there were six fugitive Mafiosi in the region: three around thirty years old, two around forty, and only one elderly man, Pasquale Villano, who was sixty-five. "To judge from the clothes in the wardrobe, the only likely candidate is this Pasquale Villano," Fazio concluded.

"That name rings a bell," said Augello. "Excuse me just a minute, while I go and check."

He got up, went out, and returned a minute later with a photograph in his hand.

"It was pinned up in the hallway with the other wanted notices," he said, putting the photo down in front of Montalbano, who looked at him and said:

"It can't be him."

"Why not?"

"Because it says here this man is four foot eleven, whereas the clothes in the wardrobe were for a man of normal stature. So this confirms that the man is not one of the fugitives from this province."

"And therefore not someone on probation and under obligation to report to his officer," said Augello.

"So he wasn't hiding to avoid being arrested by us," Fazio concluded.

"Bear in mind, however," said the inspector, "that he was hiding only in a relative sense."

"What do you mean?" asked Augello.

"I mean that there were people coming to visit him, as we know beyond a shadow of a doubt, and who came in broad daylight, taking no particular precautions. Friends or relatives who knew where he was staying."

"Now I'm wondering," said Augello, "whether he wasn't hiding so much as merely in some kind of voluntary seclusion."

"Explain what you mean."

"I'm not sure how . . . Say somebody says he'll bow out for a while, withdraw from the scene, if, in exchange, someone does something for him . . ."

"That's always possible. But then how do you explain the guns these guys were equipped with? Might there have been someone more than a little upset at the deal you say he might have made?"

"Why not? Someone who'd wanted things to turn out differently."

"I feel a big headache coming on," said Fazio.

"Well, you can imagine how my head feels because of him," said the inspector.

The phone rang.

"Chief, 'ere'd be Mr Gambabella onna line wantin'
a —"

"Put him on."

"Inspector Montalbano?"

"Yes. I'd tried to get in touch with you but —"

"I know everything and I'd like to talk to you. This
evening I could —"

"Eight-thirty OK with you?"

"Perfect, Inspector, thank you."

He hung up. The brief exchange with Gambardella
had reminded him of something.

"Do you know whether the water main building site
is still under a sequestration order?" he asked Fazio.

"No, Chief, not any more."

"So have they resumed work?"

"Not that I know of."

"So what are they waiting for?"

"I honestly don't know."

"Well, it certainly is strange. Every day they remain
closed represents a huge loss of money."

"I'll try and see if I can find anything out right
away."

"Inspector, what happened? Wha'd you do to your
head?" asked Enzo as soon as Montalbano walked into
the trattoria.

"It's nothing, don't worry about it. I slipped and
fell."

"Then how did you manage to injure both your nose
and the back of your head?"

Jesus, what a nuisance!

"I knocked first the front of my head, and then the back."

There were no more questions. Except for: "What can I get you?"

Exam over. Only four or five times in his life had he actually eaten against his will, but that day became the sixth time. And the fact that he couldn't think of an explanation for it made things worse.

Afterwards, to distract himself he decided to take his customary walk along the jetty to the lighthouse. The sun was hidden behind clouds and the sea was grey. The inspector's dark mood got even darker.

Sitting down on his usual flat rock, he lit a cigarette.

On the rock, right at the water's edge, was the inevitable crab, which he liked to tease by throwing little pebbles at it.

"I don't feel like playing today," he said. "And you'd do me a big favour if you left me alone."

The crab politely obliged him, disappearing underwater.

At that very moment, for no apparent reason, he realized why he felt in such a bad mood.

He was conducting the investigation with the same enthusiasm with which he normally signed memos in his office.

Sure, he was questioning people, visiting crime scenes, discussing the case with Fazio, and he very nearly got his head smashed open, but it was as though the real Montalbano had gone away and delegated matters to a rough copy of himself, a stand-in devoid of hunches and ideas, unable to make connections and draw conclusions, lacking energy, passion, vitality . . .

Why was this happening to him? Was it the weariness of age?

No, that couldn't possibly be the reason, because if it was, he would have realized it immediately, and his sense of honesty would have prompted him to resign at once.

So then where was the real Montalbano?

He got his answer, loud and clear, the moment he asked the question.

The real Montalbano was in Boccadasse.

At the side of a desperate, suffering woman, keeping her company, giving her comfort and love . . .

It was this constant concern, ever present like a weight bearing down on his heart and brain, that prevented him from being intellectually lucid and quick to react, ready to seize upon as little as the trembling of a leaf, to realize when two plus two does not equal four . . .

So, how are you going to get out of this, Montalbà?

By making a solemn promise to myself. That's how.

I'll grant myself one more day. Then, if I still feel this way, I'll turn everything over to Mimì Augello. Without a second thought.

And I'll go off to Boccadasse. And stay there until Livia is back to the way she used to be.

"Chief, there are rumours going around town, and for once, they're all saying the same thing."

"And what's that?"

"They're saying that the work at the building site was stopped by the authorities following a surprise visit from three inspectors of the regional administration."

"When was that?"

"To be precise, on the afternoon of the day after the body was found in the tunnel."

"Wait a second. How could they have made an inspection when the building site was still under a sequestration?"

"Only the tunnel was. And it was enough for the inspectors to see the tunnel from the outside to conclude that it was in violation of the guidelines established in the ratification of the government contract."

"And how was it supposed to be?"

"Did you see where the three pipes had been placed?"

"They were buried."

"Exactly. They were put directly into the bare earth. And they shouldn't have been. According to the contract, they were supposed to be placed inside a concrete tunnel of sufficient height to allow for repairs in the event of a break."

"And so now they're supposed to pull the pipes out, build a concrete tunnel, and then put them back in?"

"Exactly."

"So why aren't they doing that?"

"Because the Rosaspina people say it wasn't their fault, but the regional administration's, since they still hadn't paid Rosaspina the amount promised at the halfway point of the project, but only forced them to make do, to avoid losing any more time. Now, since the cost of the materials has gone up in the meantime, if they want their tunnel in concrete, the estimate goes up. But the regional government has no desire to allocate any more money."

Montalbano remained silent for a moment, thinking, then said:

"Well, it certainly is curious."

"What is?"

"The timing of the inspection."

"You think there's a connection between Nicotra's murder and the arrival of the inspectors?"

"I don't really think it. It's just a feeling."

"Care to tell us more?"

"Say two competing groups reach a secret agreement allowing for one of the two to do a certain job. The agreement rests on a precarious balance, meaning neither can afford to slip up. But then something happens that throws everything out of balance. Everything must be worked out all over again, from square one, with new rules. The inspectors sent from Palermo have . . . How shall I put it? They've frozen the situation."

"And what, in your opinion, will happen if, say, they don't reach a new agreement?"

"The two groups will go back to being enemies. Didn't I say I had the impression that some kind of negotiations were taking place? I'm convinced that in a few days we'll know what really happened. And then we'll start being able to make some moves of our own."

The telephone rang.

"'Ere'd happen a be a soitan lawyer by the name o' Nino Varbarera onna premisses, an' 'e wants a talk t'yiz poissonally in poisson."

"Wait just a second." Then, turning to Fazio: "Do you know a lawyer by the name of Nino Varbarera?"

"It must be Nino Barbera, administrative counsellor to Rosaspina, the one who recommended —"

"Yeah, I remember. OK, Cat, bring him in."

Barbera the lawyer was a rather diminutive man, well dressed and dapper, with a confident air.

After the customary polite introductions, the inspector sat him down in front of his desk and with a friendly smile waited for him to start talking.

"Inspector, I'm not sure whether you know that I am a member of the board of directors of Rosaspina Construction, the firm for which the late Gerlando Nicotra worked."

Montalbano didn't make a peep, but only kept on looking at him and smiling affably.

"I should begin by saying that it was I who insisted that Nicotra, who was already working for the company that we replaced, should stay on and work for us. I have no reason to hide the fact that I was pressured considerably to do this by the Honourable Carratello, assessor of public works and a good friend of mine. Poor Gerlando immediately showed himself to be a conscientious employee, honest, devoted, and endowed with rare abilities . . . A truly irreparable loss."

Montalbano was still smiling and not saying anything. He looked as if he was under a spell; he didn't move a muscle.

"But I'll get to the point. The company's safe is in my office. We use it not so much to store cash as to hold important documents. The only people with the keys to this safe were me and the late Nicotra. I also kept my pistol in the safe, a Beretta. I have a licence for it. Well, yesterday, when I opened the safe for the first time since poor Gerlando's death, I realized, to my great shock, that my gun was gone."

Montalbano remained immobile for a few more seconds.

Then he roused himself.

"Did you look carefully?" he asked in the most serious of tones.

"Of course!"

"And it wasn't there?"

"No, it wasn't!"

"Did you by any chance check whether it didn't end up in a drawer?"

"Yes, I did!"

"And who could have taken it?"

"I told you who had the keys, didn't I?"

But the inspector, who was having a ball, wanted to hear the lawyer himself say the name.

"Yes, but that means nothing. You could have lent the keys to someone who —"

"Out of the question."

"Then maybe the late Nicotra lent his."

"I would rule that out, too."

"Well, what is it, then?"

Finally the lawyer, pulled by the reins, made up his mind.

"I'm sorry to have to say this, but it could only have been Nicotra who took it."

"The late Nicotra," Montalbano corrected him.

"Yes, of course."

"To do what, in your opinion?"

For the first time since he'd entered, the lawyer seemed a little less self-assured.

"Well, maybe . . . and this is just something I've heard, mind you . . . anyway, there's been an insistent rumour around town that Inge, his wife — a fine-looking woman, German — had a lover . . . and so it's possible that he found out and went mad with jealousy and . . ."

"I see. So, in your opinion, he took the gun to shoot her lover?"

"I can't imagine any other motive . . ."

"Except that instead of killing his wife's lover, it was his wife's lover who killed him."

Barbera the lawyer threw up his hands and heaved a big sigh by way of resignation.

"Unfortunately, that seems to be what happened."

"Do you know something, sir? Our Forensics team recovered a cartridge case just outside the front door of the late Nicotra's house. They think poor Nicotra was killed with an Italian gun. It may in fact be your very own Beretta."

The lawyer made a dejected face. "If only I could have foreseen . . ."

"What are you going to do? That's how it happened. It's not your fault."

Montalbano started smiling affably again.

"Listen, I want you to go into another office now with Inspector Fazio and file a report on the theft of your gun. And I thank you from the bottom of my heart for your cooperation."

It took Fazio hardly any time at all to draft the report, and he returned to the inspector's office at once. There was something he wanted to ask him, a question he'd kept to himself all the while.

"Why didn't you tell him his story about the gun didn't hold water, since Nicotra already owned one?"

"Think for a minute, Fazio. Barbera came here as a kind of test, to float a trial balloon. He wanted to see how I would react, if I would swallow his story. And I pretended to do so. Now they'll make another move. Because it's clear that we're still at the opening lines of a play they want to put on. Meanwhile, however, the lawyer, without wanting to, revealed something very important to us."

"And what's that?"

"That they didn't know, and still don't know, that both the old man and Nicotra were armed."

"And where does that get us?"

"It gives us an important card to play at the right moment."

When he got home the first thing he did was phone Livia. He was afraid that if Gambardella stayed late, Livia would have already gone to bed before he had time to call her.

The telephone rang for a long time with no answer. Maybe Livia'd had a bad day and gone and buried herself under the covers after unplugging the phone and the outside world. He'd just made up his mind to hang up when he heard:

"Hello? Hello?"

It was Livia, a bit out of breath, but louder and clearer than he'd heard her sound in quite a while.

"I'm sorry, Salvo, but I was just unlocking the door when I heard the phone ring and —"

"You were out?"

"Yes. And I'm dead tired."

"Had you been out for a long time?"

"Yes. For a good four hours . . ."

He almost couldn't believe his ears. For months if she went out for even half an hour it was good going!

". . . I was running every which way. Because of Selene."

"And who's that?"

"Oh, right, I never told you."

"You named the dog Selene?"

"Yes."

"But Selene is a woman's name!"

"And Selene in fact is a female. She's a little sick at the moment, and so I took her to see two vets. I'm sorry, Salvo, but now that I think of it, do you really think I'm so stupid that I wouldn't know the significance of the name Selene?"

Wonderful! What a magnificent surprise! The particular note that signalled the start of a squabble had sounded again in Livia's voice. Would to heaven that this Selene had granted her a reprieve! Just to check, he purposely provoked her.

112

"If it had been me instead of Selene you certainly wouldn't have taken me to see two different doctors."

"Are you some kind of moron or something, comparing yourself to a dog?"

Moron! She'd called him a moron! A holy, blessed word!

Livia had made a huge recovery, there was no doubt about it.

"Just kidding, my love."

They couldn't have ended on a better note.

As soon as he hung up, the inspector was so happy he felt like doing cartwheels. Luckily he restrained himself. Otherwise, he surely would have ended up back in the hospital, needing a few more stitches in his head.

He was on his way to the kitchen to see what Adelina had cooked for him when the doorbell rang. He went to open it.

CHAPTER
NINE

They both agreed that, despite the pleasant evening weather, it would be imprudent to sit out on the veranda. Someone passing along the beach might see them.

"What happened to you?" asked Gambardella when he saw his face.

The inspector had no problem telling him everything that had happened at the hospital.

"With these sorts of methods they've scared everyone to death and created a vacuum around me," Gambardella commented. "My investigation is practically at a standstill, even though there's still a great deal to be discovered, especially after something that happened the day before yesterday."

"I know nothing about that."

"A few months ago Albachiara won the competition for the contract to build a district headquarters in the Riguccio area between Montelusa and Vigàta. Construction began fifteen days ago, but the day before yesterday work was halted."

"By whom?"

"By the regional administration."

"What was the reason?"

"No idea . . . Apparently an important clause, to be added by common agreement, was omitted, either by accident or on purpose, in Albachiara's copy of the contract."

At that moment a thought flashed through Montalbano's head like a falling star. But he was unable to stop it, and felt upset. This never used to happen to him.

But then another thing occurred to him. And he stated it at once, for fear of forgetting it in turn.

"If I remember correctly, you told me you wanted to get in touch with someone Piscopo had mentioned to you . . ."

"Yes, the former site foreman, Filippo Asciolla. Piscopo told him he was sacked by Albachiara over a difference with the superintendent and wanted to get revenge."

"Did you talk to him?"

Gambardella grimaced.

"Unfortunately I lost a few hours before I called him, and that was enough for him to find out about Piscopo. By then he realized that it was dangerous to have anything to do with me."

"What did he do?"

"He immediately ended the conversation, saying he had nothing to tell me concerning his work with Albachiara and asked me not to bother him any further."

"So, end of story?"

"Not exactly. Immediately afterwards I sent him a note in which I solemnly pledged that should he ever decide to tell me anything, I would never mention his name to anyone, and that any eventual meeting between us would remain absolutely secret."

"Did you get an answer?"

"Yes. This."

He pulled a folded sheet of paper out of his jacket pocket and handed it to the inspector. It was a photocopy.

Mr Gambardella,

I am warning you that if you do not stop incessantly calling me I will report you to the police for harassment.

You are trying to persuade me, with the promise of a lot of money, to declare something that is not true, and that is that I was dismissed by Albachiara Construction because I was not in agreement with their use of second-rate materials in the construction of the school complex in Villaseta. This is false. The cause of my dismissal was a disagreement with Engineer Riggio, the works manager, for reasons that had nothing to do with the quality of the materials.

I hope this has cleared everything up and I won't be hearing from you again.

Filippo Asciolla

"It's quite clear. I wonder who wrote it for him," Montalbano commented.

"I know he has a daughter, very pretty and a good girl, who's in her last year of high school."

"Did you offer him money?"

"Of course not."

"How many times did you call him?"

"Just once, without even mentioning why I wanted to meet him. It was him who told me he had nothing to say to me about his work with Albachiara."

"So this letter has a precise purpose. Asciolla wants it to be publicly known that he has no intention of working with you. It's a very shrewd move."

"I realized that myself. And I gave Asciolla a helping hand."

"How?"

"What you read just now is a photocopy. The original I put in my pocket this morning and went to the offices of Albachiara. As a journalist I wanted to know the reason for the work stoppage. But some sort of guard prevented me from entering because I didn't have an appointment. I protested and shouted and, pulling out my handkerchief, I let the envelope with the original letter fall out. I am positive that by now the board of directors of Albachiara have had a look at it."

"So am I. And what do you intend to do now?"

"I'm going to sit tight. I have to make it look like I've broken off all contact with Asciolla. It's up to him to make the next move."

They spoke a bit longer, Montalbano asked him about his son, and then Gambardella said goodbye.

He had just sat down at his desk when the telephone rang.

"Chief, 'ere'd a happen a be a Mr Terrazzino onna premisses 'oo'd like t' talk t' —"

"Did he tell you what he wants?"

"Wait a secon' an' I'll ax 'im."

Moments later.

"'E says as like 'e, Mr Terrazzino, 'd happen a be the owner o' the 'ouse in Rizzutello where the dead man Nicotira, the one 'at was moidered, used to live."

And what could he want? At any rate, it was best to find out.

"Show him in and get me Fazio."

Fazio and Terrazzino, who was a tiny but very well-dressed man of about sixty, came in at the same time. Fazio sat down, while Terrazzino, before settling into his chair, hitched up his trousers, holding them by the crease, and then, once seated, smoothed them out with his fingers and adjusted his jacket, tie, and glasses. Having watched him in silence all the while, Montalbano could finally open his mouth.

"From what I understand, Mr Terrazzino, you —"

"Actually, my name is Terrazzano. To be precise: Emilio Terrazzano."

"My apologies. So you're the owner of the house that Nicotra lived in with his wife?"

"Yes, sir. But, for the sake of precision, I must make it clear that I am a very precise man. I had originally let the house eight years ago to the German girl, who at the time wasn't yet married to Nicotra."

"Please explain."

"To be precise, Inge came to Vigàta when she was barely twenty years old, as the fiancée of a bricklayer

118

named Pino Pennisi. A few months later, however, she left him because she'd become the mistress of Don Gaetano Pasanisi. To be even more precise, it was Don Gaetano who set her up in the house, but to avoid gossip, he wanted the contract to be in the girl's name. Then, after Don Gaetano died six years ago, the girl found comfort at once from Nicotra, who married her."

"I see. And why, to be precise, did you come here?"

"Er, may I ask a question first, just for the sake of precision?"

"Please go ahead."

"Is it true that there has been no news of Inge and that her car was set on fire?"

"Precisely."

"Then I am here to tell you that yesterday evening I got a phone call from a lawyer in Germany who said he was speaking on Inge's behalf. The time was seven-thirty, to be precise."

Montalbano's and Fazio's eyes opened wide, and they exchanged a puzzled glance. They hadn't expected this.

"Are you sure he was calling from Germany?"

"My dear Inspector, the number that appeared on the readout was not Italian, and while the man did speak Italian, he had a very strong German accent."

"What did he want?"

"He was informing me of the cancellation of the rental contract and bringing to my attention that, as the current month had been paid in advance, I still retained in my possession the three months' rent paid as a security deposit upon the signing of the contract. He

119

said I should check the condition of the house and if I found no damage or repairs to deduct, would I please forward the money by means of a cheque made out to Inge, and send it to the lawyer's address."

"And he left you his name and address?"

"I've got them right here."

He handed the inspector a piece of paper, on which was written: *Rudolf Sterling, Esq., barrister, Wochenerstrasse 142, Bonn.*

Montalbano took down the information and gave it back to him.

"What do you intend to do?" he asked.

"I would like to know if I can go into the house and see precisely what state they left it in, and if I do find damage, assess the monetary value and subtract this from the security deposit."

"I don't think there are any legal barriers, especially if we accompany you. The problem is that there are no more keys. We'll have to —"

"Well, to be precise, I myself have a copy," said Terrazzano. "If they didn't change the lock during all these years . . ."

Montalbano made a split-second decision. "Are you free at the moment?"

"Yes."

"Let's go there right now," he said.

Halfway up the country road, the abandoned building site was an enormous blot against the greenery that over the past few days had burst forth with unstoppable force.

And this fresh, sparkling, renewed life made the building site look like an infected wound that would never heal.

That was when the idea Montalbano'd had as he was speaking to Gambardella and had been unable to bring into focus came back to him, clear and sharply defined.

"Remind me, when we get back to the station, that there's something I need to ask you about the building sites," he said, touching Fazio, who was at the wheel, on the shoulder.

They pulled up in front of Nicotra's house and got out.

Terrazzano, key already in hand, slipped it into the lock and turned. The door opened, and they went in.

Fazio opened the windows. Luckily Forensics had left everything reasonably in order.

"I need to look at everything very precisely," Terrazzano announced.

"I didn't doubt it for a minute," said Montalbano.

It took Terrazzano two hours to check everything from the taps and their related plumbing, to the toilet bowls and their drainpipes, to the ceilings and false ceilings, to the floor tiles and the state of the walls, and he did it with a fussiness that very nearly made Montalbano lose his cool.

When they all met up again on the ground floor, Montalbano felt like asking him a question.

"Just for the sake of precision, sir, did you know that the Nicotras had a guest for several months?"

"Yes. Inge told me one day when I ran into her by chance — in Via Garibaldi, to be precise."

"Did she say who it was?"

"Yes, an uncle of hers. She'd lost both her parents when she was just a girl, and this uncle had been a sort of second father to her."

Montalbano didn't know what to say. Nothing made sense any more in this affair.

"Well, I've done what I had to do. We can go now," said Terrazzano.

Fazio closed the windows again, and they went out. Terrazzano locked the door.

"All that's left for me to do is return the whole deposit," he said.

"Aren't you going to have a look at the garage?" Montalbano asked.

"The garage isn't mine. And, more precisely, I don't have the key to it."

"What do you mean, it isn't yours?"

"About six months ago Inge called me to ask for permission to build a garage for their car on the land next to the house, and I said OK, as long as they took responsibility for everything."

"About six months ago, you say. Could you be more precise?"

Terrazzano reflected for a moment, then said:

"To be absolutely precise, I'd say six and a half months ago. I'm sure of it because on that day . . ."

But Fazio and Montalbano were no longer listening to him. An exchange of glances was enough, and each knew what the other was thinking.

The arrival of the supposed uncle was what made them need to build a garage.

Montalbano looked over at the garage.

The Forensics people had raised the rolling shutter and then pulled it back down to the ground, but they had left it unlocked.

His legs began moving on their own, without waiting for his brain to give them the order.

He bent down, grabbed the handle on the door, and raised it.

All the same, there wasn't much light.

He took a step forward, felt around for the switch with his right hand, and pressed it, but no light came on.

Maybe the bulb was burnt out. He took two steps inside.

Terrazzano got into the car, since the matter, to be precise, didn't concern him. Fazio, on the other hand, went into the garage and instinctively pushed the switch.

Nothing.

He tried again twice, and finally the light came on.

There was hardly anything to see, other than a pair of tyres in a corner. On a shelf were a hammer, three screwdrivers, a pair of pliers. On the floor, a dirty rag.

The cement floor, divided into large squares, was stained with engine oil in the middle.

Fazio looked questioningly at the inspector.

Why was he standing there motionless, eyes half-closed, as though listening to a faraway song?

Then, without moving, Montalbano said softly: "Close the garage door."

Fazio obeyed.

"Turn off the light, but press the button only once."

Bewildered, Fazio did as he was told. The light did not go off.

"Now try again, but pressing twice consecutively."

The light went off.

"Now turn it on, but pressing only once." It remained dark.

"Try pressing twice."

The light returned.

Montalbano then went over to the switch, which was one of those large industrial ones covered in thick but transparent plastic. He studied it long and hard, took one step back, and continued looking at it thoughtfully. Fazio held his tongue, not wanting to disturb him.

Then Montalbano asked:

"Do you have anything with a sharp point in the car, something to make a hole in the wall?"

"No."

The inspector cursed.

"However," Fazio continued, "on that shelf there's a hammer and three screwdrivers. We can try."

"Then bring me the torch you always keep in the car, but without letting Terrazzano see you do so. And tell him to hang on a little longer; we should be done in about fifteen minutes."

When Fazio returned, Montalbano asked him for the torch and told him to lower the garage door and turn off the light with the method they'd discovered.

Then he turned on the torch.

"What are you looking for?" asked Fazio.

"As you can see, the electricity cables are trunked and chased into the wall. But when a wall is poorly plastered like this one, the outline of the trunking begins to emerge. Now, if we start at the switch and follow a straight line up, we should be able . . ."

"There it is," Fazio said suddenly.

"Where?" asked Montalbano.

"There's a kind of strip about an inch wide that starts roughly six or seven inches before the wall meets the roof."

The inspector couldn't see anything.

Damn old age! But this was no time to get depressed.

"Could I have the torch?" asked Fazio.

Montalbano handed it to him. What, after all, was the point of him hanging on to it?

"Up on the ceiling you can see the whole strip, up to the hole where the cable comes out."

"Excellent. Have you worked out why the strip becomes more visible as it gets closer to the roof?"

"Yes, because there's more humidity there."

"Right. Shall we make a bet?"

"First you have to tell me what we're betting on."

"That we'll find a second strip of trunking, but this time at the opposite end, where the wall meets the floor."

"No, I'll pass on that bet."

He pointed the beam downwards, and a moment later said:

"There it is! I see the strip!"

Montalbano bent down to look. The strip started to become visible about three inches above the floor and then disappeared.

"Get the hammer and screwdriver and remove the plaster over the strip, but carefully, as gently as possible, otherwise you risk cutting the light cable."

Five minutes later, a piece of typically flexible sheath of the kind used to encase electrical wires appeared.

"I wonder what this other installation is for," said Fazio.

"Can't you imagine?"

"No."

"It's for the light in the basement."

Fazio looked stunned.

"Are you telling me there's a basement under here?"

"To be precise, yes."

"Where's the entrance?"

"That is the question. Do something for me. Take Terrazzano into town and then come straight back here."

He went out with Fazio to say goodbye to Terrazzano, then watched Fazio shoot off like a rocket. He went back into the garage.

Use your brains, Salvo. With one push, the switch turns on the light in the basement, with two, the light in the garage . . .

And what if the same switch opened and closed the basement entrance as well?

126

CHAPTER
TEN

This was a plausible hypothesis, yet to be verified.

For there was one thing he was sure of, which was that the controls to the basement entrance could not be inside the house. It would not have escaped the careful examination of the Forensics team, nor Terrazzano's precision inspection.

Thus, before getting down to work, he wanted to check the garage walls inch by inch to see whether there wasn't some sort of hidden button.

He found nothing.

He remembered how nice and convenient it was when, as a child, he believed in the existence of a magical formula that uncovered hidden doors and made them open.

Open sesame . . .

Just to leave no stone unturned, half joking and half pretending — and all the while feeling ridiculous and even a little ashamed — he uttered the magic words aloud.

No hidden door miraculously opened.

And so he went over to the switch, held his index finger on it, and began his search.

Three clicks in a row: nothing. Four: still nothing.

Five: still nothing.

When he got to ten, he stopped.

No, that wasn't the answer. Anyway, say somebody was in a hurry to get down into the basement, he couldn't waste ten minutes going *click click click* with the switch.

He had to think about this.

He went out of the garage and set fire to a cigarette.

Turning it all over and over in his head, he came to the conclusion that his only choice was to remove the plastic covering and open up the switch to see how it was made and how many electrical wires ran into it.

He got back down to work with renewed enthusiasm.

The plastic covering was not attached to the switch frame as he'd thought, but was actually a sort of snap-on lid that you could remove with two fingers.

He took it off.

Removing the switch from the wall not only would have served no purpose, it would also have made his examination more difficult. To open it, one had to unscrew four screws.

The screwdriver Fazio had used was too big. Montalbano went and got another off the shelf.

He gave it a try. It would do.

He unscrewed the first screw, but as he was pulling it out from its hole to put it in his pocket, it slipped from his fingers and fell onto the floor, landing a few inches from his left foot.

Keeping his right hand, with the screwdriver, pressed up against the switch mechanism, he crouched down, bending at the knee, to pick it up.

At that exact moment he noticed that under the involuntary pressure of his right hand, the upper part of the switch mechanism had shifted a little.

He remained in that position, puzzled and not moving. How could it have moved if there were still three screws holding it in place? Were they there only for show?

He stood up, never minding the screw that had fallen.

Once again he pressed lightly on the switch mechanism with his palm, and this time he clearly noticed that the entire upper part had again shifted slightly.

So he pressed harder, to move the upper part clockwise.

It turned all the way until it was upside down.

And then it stopped and made a sort of clicking sound. A second later, the floor under his feet started vibrating. Frightened, he leapt high in the air to one side.

Slowly, and without making the slightest sound, one of the large cement squares in the flooring, specifically the one closest to the wall with the switch on it, began to rise, revealing itself to be a trapdoor.

When it reached a vertical position, it stopped.

Montalbano bent over to look very carefully, fearing that an armed man might come up from below.

He could see the top of an iron ladder, and solid darkness below.

He reached out with one hand and touched, just once, the upside-down switch.

A very bright light came on in the basement. He looked below again.

Now he could see the entire iron ladder. It was almost vertical and attached to the wall by two iron braces, and must have been at least ten feet long.

The bit of basement flooring he was able to see was also made of dense concrete.

The curiosity to see what was down there was eating him alive, but he was scared to death to descend alone.

The potential surprises were many, all of them dangerous. What if the trapdoor closed while he was down below?

Was there another switch to open it again?

And if there was, did it work the same way as the one up above?

And if there wasn't, and the opening mechanism was completely different, would he be able to discover it before he died from lack of air?

Then he found a sort of half solution.

He took his mobile phone out of his jacket pocket and put it in a pocket of his trousers. Then he took off his jacket, folded it three times, and placed it along the edge of the trap. That way, the lid wouldn't be able to close entirely, leaving him a chance to breathe at the top of the iron ladder and to call out to Fazio when he heard him return.

Then he turned around and, gripping the ladder, face to the wall, started descending.

He touched the bottom.

Turning around, he couldn't believe his eyes.

He found himself in a small room about ten feet square.

Three walls were covered in masonry and plastered, but the fourth wall, the one opposite the iron ladder, consisted mostly of the enormous steel door of a safe.

A safe exactly like the ones you see in movies, with locks, handles, and combination knobs.

The door was slightly ajar.

Recovering from his shock, the inspector, using both hands, opened it all the way.

The inside was entirely covered with shelving, and was six feet wide and three feet deep.

And completely empty.

What could it have contained?

But as soon as he asked himself the question, he realized that by staying there, looking around inside the safe, he was just wasting his time.

He climbed back out, stood aside, picked up his jacket, and turned the switch round.

The lid closed again, as before without making the slightest sound. He put the plastic cover back over the switch, then turned off the light in the basement and in the garage, went outside, and pulled down the garage door.

He looked at his watch. Almost one o'clock.

He took out his phone and dialled Jannaccone's number.

"What is it, Inspector?"

"What were you doing?"

Surprised by the question, Jannaccone didn't answer immediately.

"I was . . . on my way to lunch."

"Then I'll call back in an hour or so."

He was just pretending. He knew Jannaccone wouldn't let go.

"Not at all, Inspector, tell me what you wanted."

"I'm just curious. When you searched the Nicotras' house, did you also look in the garage?"

"Of course."

"And you didn't find anything?"

"No, nothing. Why do you ask?"

"Because for my part I found a little something."

"Oh, really? What?"

"A basement with a giant safe in it."

"Fuck!"

"Exactly."

"I'll be right over with the team."

"No, go and have your lunch in peace. There's no hurry any more. We'll meet at three."

Then he immediately rang Fazio. "Where are you?"

"On my way back. I'll be there in about ten —"

"Listen, I've finished here, and I'm going to head off on foot to the old lady's illegal cafe. Meet me there."

In all likelihood the old lady was a good cook, and he was in the throes of some serious hunger pangs.

He got to the shop just as Fazio was pulling up behind him, having obviously flown there.

"What did you find?"

"Big stuff. But this isn't the place to discuss it. For now let's concentrate on eating."

They went in and sat down at a table already set for two.

The old woman came out of the kitchen, looked at them, recognized them, and frowned.

"Our deal din't say you could come an stuff your guts."

"Whoever said we didn't want to pay? We're going to pay, don't you worry about that. What have you got that's good?"

"Homemade tagliatelle with sauce."

"Sounds good," the two men said in unison.

"An' f'r a secon' course, rabbit *cacciatore.*"

"Sounds good," the chorus repeated.

"An' wha' kinda wine you want? Drinkable or good?"

"Good," said the little chorus.

Before they attacked their tagliatelle, the other two tables were filled. The old lady did brisk business.

They ate well, and paid eleven euros a head.

"I feel like taking out a membership to this place," Fazio said as they were leaving.

Outside, they saw something they weren't expecting. Leaning with his buttocks against their car was Pitrineddru, the old woman's forty-year-old colossus of a son, looking at them with his arms crossed.

"You think he wants to make trouble?" Fazio asked softly.

"I don't think so, but stay on the alert anyway. The gorilla's capable of anything."

When they were in front of him, Pitrineddru remained immobile, not budging an inch.

"We'll be needing to get into our car," Fazio said politely. "If you would just step aside . . ."

"No."

"Why not?"

"Ya gotta tell me somethin' first."

"What do you want to know?" Montalbano intervened.

"Didja find Inghi?"

As he was saying the German woman's name, he cast a quick glance at the door of his mother's shop. He was afraid she might come out and catch him talking to the police. But that glance revealed a lot to the inspector.

"If I tell you something, will you tell me something, too?"

"OK."

"Apparently Inge went back to Germany."

Pitrineddru hung his head down to his chest and muttered something.

"What did you say?"

Pitrineddru raised his head and looked at them. To their shock, Montalbano and Fazio saw that he had tears in his eyes.

"I said, 'Better alive than dead.'"

"Did you love Inge?" Montalbano asked.

Pitrineddru nodded.

"Did you and her make love?"

Another nod.

"When?"

"Sometime she'd call an' wanted the groceries delivered to her house, an' I'd deliver them."

"And where did you do it?"

"Wherever she wanted. In the garage, in the living room . . ."

At this point, with tears now streaming down his face, he ran away behind the house . . .

Since there was still time before Forensics arrived, and Fazio was itching to see the underground safe with his own eyes, Montalbano decided to make him happy, and they went into the garage and lowered the door behind them.

When Fazio came back up through the trapdoor, and Montalbano closed the lid, they went back outside.

Fazio was clearly stunned.

"Until now the secret underground bunkers I'd seen were used to hide fugitives. This one's something else altogether. What do you think they kept in the safe?"

"I don't even want to think about it. I only hope Jannaccone can tell us with some certainty."

"One thing is clear. That Nicotra wasn't just an accountant for Rosaspina."

"Yeah."

"Why are you so quiet?" Fazio asked him.

"Because I'm unable to get an overall picture of things. I haven't had time to think it all through. Too many new developments, too many cards being played. This morning we learned that Inge is supposedly alive and in Germany, and that the man with the gloves was her uncle . . . Is it true? Or is it a red herring? What were the Nicotras' responsibilities, uncle included, concerning the safe in the basement? Were they simply guarding it? Or did they know the combination to open and close it? And why was the house attacked? To take what was in the safe? Or was the safe already empty? As you can see, a lot of pieces are still missing from the overall puzzle."

"They're here," said Fazio.

There were two cars. Jannaccone bolted out of the first one. He'd brought three men with him.

Montalbano said it was better if they all went into the garage together, even if it was a bit tight. That way they wouldn't arouse the curiosity of anyone passing by.

Once they were all inside, he lowered the door, turned on the light, and explained to Jannaccone how the light switch worked.

Jannaccone wanted to try for himself and opened the lid of the trapdoor.

"Down below," said the inspector, "there is a large, empty safe. What I want to know is what was inside it. See if you can work that out."

"We'll work it out," Jannaccone promised.

"Fazio and I'll let you get on in peace. But bear in mind: it's extremely important that nobody knows that we discovered this basement. I mean it."

He didn't have time to finish his sentence before Jannaccone started going down the ladder.

"Stop at the building site," Montalbano said to Fazio as soon as they headed off.

Five minutes later they pulled up and Montalbano got out. "You wait in the car," he said to Fazio.

The dried mud was no longer a solid, continuous surface. It was riddled with hundreds of crevices like open gashes. And inside these crevices the green grass was beginning to sprout again.

This was what he'd wanted to see.

And he felt reassured. He got back into the car. Fazio looked at him but said nothing. And he drove off.

"I need you to do me a favour," Montalbano said to Fazio as they were going into the office.

"Whatever you say."

The inspector looked for a sheet of paper on his desk, found it, and handed it to him.

"Here's the name and address of the German lawyer. You need to find me the telephone number. If I were to ask Catarella, he would end up driving me insane or hook me up with some number in Lapland."

Fazio went out, then returned ten minutes later. "Here you go."

He'd written the phone number under the address.

Montalbano turned on the speakerphone and dialled it.

A male voice answered on the first ring and poured out a string of words among which the inspector thought he heard the lawyer's surname.

"I'd like to speak to Rudolf Sterling."

"Speaking," the man replied in Italian.

"Ah, good. This is Inspector Montalbano of the Italian police speaking. Good afternoon."

"Goot afternoon. Vot vould you like to know?"

"Was it you who phoned Mr Terrazzano in Vigàta on behalf of your client Inge Schneider?"

"Yes."

"I would like to know if I could ask you a few questions about this woman."

The lawyer hesitated a few moments before answering. "You may do so, but I may not answer."

"I certainly won't ask you anything that would remotely require you to violate your oath of professional secrecy . . ."

"Not because secret."

"Then why?"

"Because I know fery little about this voman. Inge Schneider come to my office the first time chust tree days ago."

"So that was the first time you ever saw her?"

"Yes."

"Have you been able to verify in any way that this woman was actually Inge Schneider?"

"I don't understant."

"Did you ask her to show any documents confirming her identity?"

"No. Why shouldt I do dad? She said me her name, gave me telephone numper . . ."

From his perspective, the lawyer was right.

"Could you describe her for me?"

"Vell . . . She had nothing unusual about her . . . Tall, blont, about tirty years olt . . ."

How many millions of tall, blonde, thirty-year-old women were there in Germany, anyway?

"A final question, sir. Could you give me the telephone number she left with you?"

"Yes, of course. One moment."

Fazio found a piece of paper and a pen. The lawyer dictated the number, and Fazio wrote it down.

"Can I ask why questions?" the lawyer asked.

Montalbano pretended not to have heard. "Thank you for your courtesy. Have a good day." And he hung up.

He sat there, lost in thought.

Fazio handed him the piece of paper. "If you want to call her . . ."

But the inspector seemed doubtful.

"It's not so easy. Say she lives in a boarding house, and they answer in German. I won't understand a thing."

"Shall I get Martorana for you?" Fazio suggested.

He was an officer who'd lived in Germany with his father until he was thirteen.

"OK."

"I explained everything to him," said Fazio, returning with Martorana.

"Go ahead and dial," said Montalbano, putting the speakerphone back on, in case it was Inge who answered.

But the voice they heard was a man's.

He and Martorana spoke a little, then the officer, while remaining on the line, explained to the inspector that the number they'd been given belonged to a bar where Inge Schneider had gone to find out whether there'd been any calls for her. And so the man at the bar wanted their telephone number so he could give it to Inge, in case she wanted to call back.

"No," said the inspector. "Thank him and hang up."

Martorana saluted and left.

CHAPTER
ELEVEN

"Would you please explain why you didn't want to give him our number?"

"Because, seeing that the country code is for Italy, and the area code is for Vigàta, Inge wouldn't take long to work out that we're the ones looking for her."

"Wouldn't that be better?"

"Better for us, perhaps, but not for her."

"What do you mean?"

"If Inge somehow managed to get away from her kidnappers, the first thing she should have done was to come here, to the police. Which she didn't do. A sign that she wanted to remain at large. Why? There could be any number of reasons. For example, it might be a condition imposed on her by her kidnappers for setting her free: no contact with police. And that's why I don't want her to know we're after her."

He paused, then added: "Assuming it's the real Inge."

Fazio looked a little surprised. "You have doubts?"

"Just think along with me for a second. Before Terrazzano came here, we were overwhelmingly convinced that Inge was being held by the people who murdered her husband and torched her car. Right?"

"Right."

"Then we learned — first from Terrazzano, then from the German lawyer — that Inge is free in Germany. Aside from the fact that we still don't know how she got there, who gave her the travel money, and so on along those lines, I now ask myself: after everything that happened — the break-in, her husband's murder, her kidnapping — how is it that, once out of harm's way, the first thing she thinks of is to call a lawyer to get back the security deposit on her house? Is that a normal way to act, in your opinion?"

"No."

"But let's assume it's all true, that Inge is free in Germany and wants her deposit back. Can you tell me what need there was for her to do it through a lawyer? Wouldn't it have been a whole lot simpler for her to phone Terrazzano herself?"

"You're right. Why didn't she call him herself?"

"There can only be one answer to your question: because Terrazzano knows the sound of Inge's voice quite well."

"You're right again."

"In conclusion, the likelihood that this Inge is a fake Inge is, unfortunately, a little too great."

"But what could be the reason? Why go through all the song and dance of getting in touch with someone in Germany, finding a woman who looks like Inge, sending her to a lawyer . . ."

"I'm starting to get an idea why. But it's so far-fetched, so off-the-wall that at the moment I don't even feel like talking about it."

"Please, Chief. I'll keep it to myself."

"Fazio, I'm getting more and more the feeling that in conducting this investigation, we, without knowing it, are handling a bomb. And those guys know we have a bomb on our hands, but they won't tell us, and neither do they want it to blow up."

"And so?"

"In my opinion, but it's just an impression, they're trying to move the goalposts by putting on this big production — of which, however, we've only seen the first two acts so far."

"And what would they be?"

"Don't you understand?"

"No."

"The first act was to make us believe that Nicotra got hold of Barbera's pistol for the purpose of killing his wife's lover, but the opposite happened. The second act was supposed to convince us that Inge is alive and well and back in her native Germany. Do you remember the film called *The Pizza Triangle*? These people are trying to put on something similar. Somebody from around here once wrote that the only cause of death in Sicily is adultery."

"And what's in the third act?"

"I don't know and I don't want to know. I'm neither the author nor the director of this play, but only a spectator who nevertheless has the right, at a certain point, to say exactly what he thinks about the whole thing, and whether he approves or disapproves."

"So what are we going to do in the interval between the second and third acts? Go outside for a smoke?"

142

"There are one or two small things we could do."

"Tell me one."

"Remember when we were driving out to the house with Terrazzano and I told you to remind me that there was something I wanted to talk to you about?"

"Yeah, you're right, I'm sorry, but with all that happened . . ."

"It's something you can do without leaving the comfort of your office. I just need some simple information. I want to know how many building sites, run by which companies, have been shut down by the regional government in the province of Montelusa since Nicotra's death."

Fazio looked confused. He was about to ask a question but decided not to.

"I'll start at once," he said.

The inspector was getting up to return home when Mimì Augello came into his office.

"Well, look who we have here! Care to tell me where you've been all afternoon?" the inspector asked.

"Leave me alone. There was a terrible family fight with knives drawn . . ."

"Over money?"

"These horrible family quarrels are always over money! This time we have the case of a girl, an orphan, brought into the house by an uncle, her late father's brother. The girl then gets married to a man the uncle doesn't like, and so —"

"So the fight was between the uncle and the niece?"

"Yes," said Mimì.

Then he resumed his story.

But Montalbano was no longer listening, lost in a thought that had suddenly occurred to him.

All at once he stood up.

"I'm sorry, Mimì, but I have to go."

And he raced out, leaving behind a bewildered Augello, went down to the car park, got in his car, and drove off to Pizzutello.

In the hope that the old woman's shop-restaurant was also open in the evening.

He slowed down as he approached the Nicotras' house.

Jannaccone's cars were no longer there. The garage door was pulled down, and the Forensics team had put a padlock on it. Good idea.

The sun had set. It was a quiet evening, and darkness was falling.

He drove past the shop without stopping.

It was open and he was even able to see a few people sitting at a table inside.

Moments later he did a U-turn and went back, stopping about twenty yards past it.

He got out, walked a short distance, then saw a footpath that led behind the house.

He came to a large farmyard with a stall of goats, a chicken coop, and a big fenced-in pen that served as a rabbit hutch.

Pitrineddru's giant silhouette was pacing back and forth inside the chicken coop.

Montalbano approached and called to him softly.

"Pitrineddru!"

The big man stopped and hunched slightly forward, peering into the darkness, shading his eyes with one hand.

"Whoozat?"

"It's Inspector Montalbano. The man you talked to after lunch."

"Oh," said Pitrineddru.

He came out of the chicken coop and approached him. "Is Inghi back?" he asked hopefully.

"No, not yet. But as soon as she gets back, I'll let you know."

"Promise?"

"Promise. Want a cigarette?"

Pitrineddru sighed.

"I'd like one but my mama don't want me to smoke. Not even ousside o' the house. Says iss bad for my lungs."

"C'mon, just take one and smoke it with me. Anyway, right now your mama can't see me."

Pitrineddru took his first drag with satisfaction, keeping the cigarette hidden inside his cupped hand.

"If Mama sees me she'll slap me around pretty bad."

He gave a giggle that sounded rather donkeylike, took a second puff, and then asked:

"Whattya doin' here?"

"I wanted to ask you a few questions."

"Go ahead."

"Were you aware that Inge had an uncle of hers eating and sleeping at her house?"

"Yessir."

"How did you find out?"

"Inghi tol' me and warned me not to tell nobody 'bout it, not even my mama."

"Why didn't she want anyone to know?"

"Dunno."

"But when you made love with her, where was the uncle?"

"He was always in the room upstairs. 'E never come downstairs. An' we din't make no noise."

"So you never saw him?"

The giant seemed uneasy. "Nah."

He didn't know how to lie. His "nah" came out nasal and false.

"So you can't tell me anything about him?"

"One time I heard him talkin' on 'is mobile phone. 'E was still upstairs but 'e was pissed off and yellin'."

"And what was he speaking?"

Pitrineddru was stumped by the question.

"Wha'ss he asposta be speakin'? He was speakin' words."

"No, I wanted to know whether he was speaking in German."

"Nah, 'e was talkin' juss like you an' me's talkin' now."

Montalbano, who hadn't forgotten Pitrineddru's lie, returned to the subject.

"But you never saw his face?"

Pitrineddru did a sort of bear-dance, balancing first on one foot, then the other.

"Want another cigarette?" asked the inspector.

"OK."

Montalbano lit it for him.

146

And he patiently waited for him to decide to start talking.

"I saw him once. But . . ."

"But?"

"Promiss me you won't say anything to Inghi when she comes back."

"I promise."

"One day when I wanted her I brought 'er 'er groceries wittout waitin' for 'er call. An' I saw 'er bike ousside the front door, an' 'at meant she's a' home. So I went in, bu' she wasn't downstairs. So I leff the groceries onna table an' tippytoed up the stairs so I cou' call 'er wittout 'er uncle 'earin' me. You cou' see the uncle's room wittout havin' a climb the stairs, an' so 'ass 'ow I's able a see Inghi nekkid an' on 'er knees wit' 'er 'ead between 'er uncle's legs, an' 'e's nekkid too an' sittin' onna edge o' the bed."

"Did he see you?"

"Nah, 'e cou'n't see me 'cause 'is 'ead was all bent backward."

"And what did you do?"

"Wha' could I do? I went back to the shop."

"Were you angry?"

"Yeah."

"Why didn't you take it up with Inge?"

"'Cause afterwards I thought, well, the guy's 'er uncle, after all. 'Ese kinda things 'appen a lot inna family an' nobody ge'ss upset."

"Do you remember what this man looked like?"

Pitrineddru resumed his bear-dance in his effort to remember.

"Wait . . . Wait . . . OK, OK, now iss comin' back to me . . . 'E looked about sixty an' din't 'ave no hair on 'is 'ead, but 'e had a moustache an' 'e wore white gloves an 'e had a pitcher on 'is left arm."

"A tattoo?"

"Yeah, juss like you said."

"A picture of what?"

"It was the sun wit' iss rays around it, but the sun had a man's face."

"Can you remember anything else?"

"Nah, nothin'. Bu' you'll lemme know right away when Inghi comes back?"

"I'll let you know immediately. Listen, you can have my pack of cigarettes. But you better hide it well."

On his way home he felt like a hunter with his game bag full at the end of the party.

Once indoors, he rang Augello.

"Mimì, I wanted to apologize for leaving you in the lurch."

Augello remained silent.

Montalbano thought perhaps they'd been cut off, and started yelling desperately.

"Hello! Hello!"

"I'm right here," said Mimì. "I was just recovering from the shock. You apologizing to me is a pretty rare event, you know. Even an earthquake affects me less."

"I also wanted to thank you."

"You want to give me a heart attack?! Thank me for what?"

"For an idea you gave me. Good night."

Immediately afterwards he called Livia.

"How are you?"

"Do you know what Selene did today?" Livia asked, all excited, instead of answering the question.

"No. Tell me."

God, was it wonderful to hear Livia back to being her usual self!

She went on to talk for ten minutes straight about the same subject: Selene. Only at the end did she remember him.

"And how are you?"

"Almost all better. The stitches are coming out tomorrow."

There was a moment of silence. "What stitches?"

Damn it all! Why did he say that? To compete with the dog?

"Just a little thing, nothing really . . ."

"No, don't get me all worried. Tell me."

"Well, I slipped and . . ."

"Why didn't you tell me anything?"

The tone in Livia's voice heralded the start of a squabble.

And a half squabble did occur. A half squabble that made the inspector happy.

Afterwards, his happiness was redoubled by what he found in the kitchen.

And since, when he had finished, it was time for the ten o'clock news, he turned on the TV, tuning into TeleVigàta. Ragonese the newsreader was speaking.

. . . two leaks that have come to our attention from reliable sources. The first is that Nicotra supposedly got his hands on a pistol that had been kept in the office safe. What for, we ask ourselves, if not for the purpose of killing his wife's lover, or perhaps both of them, caught in flagrante delicto? The second is that Inge Schneider, Nicotra's wife, is supposedly in Germany. Which lends credence to the thesis we put forth in the days immediately following the crime. Namely, that we are dealing with a case of marital infidelity that unfortunately ended in violence, but where the victim was the husband, disarmed by the lover who shot him in self-defence, or accidentally. Regrettably, as far as we know, Inspector Montalbano of the Vigàta police has steadfastly refused to take such a thesis into consideration, wasting his time and our money as taxpayers in pursuit of who knows what bizarre fantasies . . .

Ragonese had actually given a sort of synopsis of the prior episodes.

And this meant that the interval was over, and the third act was about to begin.

Montalbano changed the channel.

He happened upon a bicycle race taking place in very fine rain.

There was one solitary cyclist ahead of everyone else.

A voice off-camera said: *Bartoletti is leading the pack . . .*

150

The expression struck him like a cudgel straight to his forehead.

Leading the pack. What if Nicotra . . .

What if Nicotra had gone into the tunnel not to hide from whoever shot him but to lead the pack in there — the pack being his playmates, or maybe even the police?

As if to say: the truth of my death is to be found here, at the building site.

And if that was the way it was, it was confirmation of the idea, though vague, confused, uncertain, which had been knocking about in the inspector's head for a while . . .

The next morning he got into his car and drove off to Montelusa Hospital to get his stitches taken out.

Then he headed over to Montelusa Central Police. He pulled up in front of a cafe that was for all intents and purposes the police cafe and rang Jannaccone from his mobile.

"I was just on my way to see you," said Jannaccone.

"But I'm already in Montelusa."

"Then come on over."

"No, I wouldn't want to run into . . ."

"He's not coming in today."

"OK, I'll be right over."

He parked the car properly, got out in a hurry, and ten minutes later was standing in front of Jannaccone.

There was no need for him to open his mouth.

"It didn't take us very long to work out what had been in the safe," Jannaccone announced to him. "We found a lot of tiny fragments of paper money."

"Euros?"

"Yes."

"Authentic?"

"Yes. Just think, there were fragments on every single shelf. There must have been millions and millions of euros in there."

"Dirty money."

"I agree."

"Fingerprints?"

"Yes. A man's."

"Were you able —"

"Yes, they were his, Inspector," Jannaccone said, smiling. And he continued, "Do you remember those very clear footprints the two men who broke in had left inside the house?"

"Of course."

"We found the same footprints, less clearly delineated, in the basement room, outside the safe."

"So it would be logical to assume that in addition to killing Nicotra and kidnapping his wife and their elderly guest, the two men also made off with the money?"

"So it would seem."

"About this safe, incidentally . . . the less said, the better . . ."

Jannaccone understood at once.

"Well, sooner or later I'm going to have to write my report for the commissioner just the same."

"Is it pressing?"

"No, I can wait four or five days . . ."

"Thanks."

"Oh," said Jannaccone, "I also thought it was best to padlock the garage door. Here are the keys."

CHAPTER
TWELVE

After telling Fazio and Augello what he'd learned first from Pitrineddru and then Jannaccone, Montalbano wanted to know what they thought.

But Augello, who at a certain point started to look distracted, came out with a question instead.

"Could you repeat your description of the tattoo?"

"Pitrineddru said it was a sun with rays and that the sun had a man's face. On his left arm."

Augello remained silent, with a faraway look in his eyes.

"I can't read your mind, you know," said the inspector.

"I'm sorry," said Augello, "but I'm positive I saw that tattoo a few years ago . . . but I can't remember where I saw it or who the man was who had it."

"Really?" said Montalbano. "If you could somehow manage to recover that memory, it would be like winning the lottery."

"It's better if we forget about it for the time being, because the more I try to force myself, the worse it is. At any rate, if you want to know my opinion, I'll only say that I think we finally have a motive for the whole affair."

"And what would that be?"

"Stealing the money from the safe."

"Think so?"

"I'm convinced."

"How did it go, in your opinion?"

"Well, the two men break into the house, surprising everyone in their sleep, and while one man keeps his gun trained on the old man and Inge, the other forces Nicotra to go down into the garage basement, get the money, and put it in three or four large sacks. Then —"

"Too risky," Fazio interrupted him.

"How so?" asked Augello.

"Just two men, for an operation like that, doesn't seem like enough to me."

"Especially," said the inspector, "since Jannaccone said they found the footprints of the same two as in the house, but no tracks from any bare feet, as there should have been if Nicotra had gone down there. Anyway, who, in the meantime, was going to keep an eye on Inge and the so-called uncle?"

"Couldn't they have tied them up together and gagged them before going to the garage?"

"That's always possible. But at this point," said Montalbano, "we must ask ourselves the question: who exactly were these thieves?"

"What are you getting at?"

"I doubt they were common thieves of the sort that burgle homes or stage hold-ups. This was a big deal. They were there to steal a sum of money greater than you would find in all the banks of Vigàta put together. They went there with absolute certainty, because they knew about the hidden safe. So, how many people knew this secret? Certainly fewer than you can count on two hands."

"And what does this mean?"

"It means it might have been a commissioned robbery. The thieves weren't professional, but they were acting on behalf of a third party. The victims of the theft will discover sooner or later who sent them. So somebody gets killed. Shall we change the subject?"

And, turning to Fazio: "Got any news for me?"

Fazio dug a piece of paper out of his jacket pocket and read it.

"Chief, there are six building sites that have been shut down by the regional administration, and these six are owned by Rosaspina, Albachiara, Soledoro, Lo Schiavo, Spampinato, and Farullo."

"Give me the piece of paper."

Fazio gave it to him, and the inspector sat there a moment perusing it. Then he asked:

"The firm that started the work on the water main is called Primavera, right?"

"Yes."

"But Primavera, Rosaspina, and the others — are these surnames or just made-up names?"

"Just made-up names, Chief. Whereas Lo Schiavo, Spam —"

"Are surnames, yeah, I got that."

He was suddenly overcome with a desire to see one of these dormant building sites.

"Aside from the Rosaspina site, which is the closest one to us?"

"The Albachiara site. It's in Riguccio."

"Now I need you to do another search. I want to know who the heads of these six companies are."

"I've got the names for Rosaspina and have already told you them. For the others I'm going to need a few days."

"OK, but don't take too long." He adjourned the meeting.

He left the office an hour earlier than usual, because he wanted to go and see the shut-down site of the Albachiara firm, which, as the journalist Gambardella had told him, had won the contract to build an administrative building.

On his way to the Riguccio district, he wondered where this strong urge had come from and realized that he'd been unable to get out of his head the hunch he'd had the previous night — that is, that by going and dying inside the tunnel, Nicotra was trying to say something.

When he'd woken up that morning, he'd noticed that it promised to be another day of bad weather. The sky was darkening. And now it was raining hard.

Arriving at the building site, he pulled up but stayed inside the car. It was raining too hard to get out. He would have got soaked.

The site consisted of just three earth movers parked in a huge, empty open space at the foot of a hill, much of which had slid down to the bottom, owing to the heavy rain that had been falling.

But there was something else Montalbano couldn't understand, since his windscreen wipers didn't work very well. Off to the left side of the open space stood a structure, made perhaps of concrete, all in one block. It was about fifty feet high and looked like a pyramid.

What could be the purpose of that?

He put the car in gear and drove up to it, opening the door to get a better look.

Then he understood.

They'd moved all the mud out of the open area and made a mound of it, but much of the still-liquid mud had slid down to the ground, leaving a pyramidal form that had eventually dried.

The inspector gazed at it, spellbound. A pyramid of mud.

The perfect representation, at once concrete and symbolic, of everything that, little by little, was becoming clearer in his head.

And he wondered whether it wasn't Nicotra who, like the solitary cyclist, had led him there.

By the time he got to the trattoria the rain had turned into a proper thunderstorm. His visit to the building site and the day's weather had taken away his appetite.

He went in and found only two regulars and the television turned on.

Nicolò Zito, the Free Channel newsman and Montalbano's friend, was on the screen, talking.

He said that with the almost simultaneous closing of six building sites in Montelusa province, a very serious situation had developed. That day, a delegation of unpaid construction workers in danger of losing their jobs had been received by the prefect, who had promised to intervene at once on their behalf with the regional administration in the hope of ending the work stoppage as soon as the firms in question brought themselves in line with the regulations.

Enzo came out to take his order. But he wasn't his usual self and looked troubled.

"Anything wrong?" the inspector asked him.

"I'm worried about my brother-in-law, 'Ntonio, who's got three kids and fears he might lose his job."

"What does he do?"

"He's a surveyor with Farullo Construction, which had to shut down their building site in Sicudiana."

Montalbano's ears pricked up. Enzo continued.

"They've started talking about reducing personnel if this rain keeps up much longer."

"Do you know why the regional inspector —"

"That's just it," Enzo interrupted him.

"What do you mean?"

"My brother-in-law swears to God that no inspector ever came to his building site. The firm's bosses say they had to stop work by order of the inspectors, but they're lying. Anyway, 'Ntonio says everything's by the book at his site."

"So how do you explain it?"

"There is no explanation."

"I'd like to talk to your brother-in-law. If it's not too much trouble for him, think he could come to my office around three?"

"I'll call him right now and ask."

Enzo returned five minutes later.

"He says OK, he'll be there at three. So, what can I get you?"

The inspector ate hardly anything, to Enzo's great displeasure.

When he left the trattoria he got soaked. The water was coming down in torrents, and a powerful, angry wind made it almost impossible to walk. The sewage drains were throwing up liquid and the pavements were underwater.

'Ntonio Garzullo was a slender, bespectacled man of about forty, rather shabbily dressed and quite nervous.

"Inspector, it was really stupid as hell for Enzo to go and tell you about what I said when I was just letting off steam in the bosom of the family," he began, drying his head with a handkerchief.

"Enzo knew perfectly well he wasn't talking to a police inspector, but to a friend. And you should know it, too. Now the two of us are going to have a nice little private chat, and nobody will ever know anything about it."

'Ntonio seemed somewhat reassured. And he was keen to explain why he'd spoken as he had.

"Because, you see, if even a hint of what I said reaches the ears of the Farullo bosses, I'm finished."

"Nothing will reach their ears, I assure you."

"Tell me what you wanted to know."

"First of all, are you absolutely sure that the regional inspectors never came?"

"Yes, sir, I am. As sure as death. I was always at the site from morning to evening. They never set foot there. And they never came to any of the offices, either."

"But then how did you find out that the order to stop work came from the regional administration?"

"The engineer Gangitano, the site manager, told us himself. He brought us all together to give us the news."

"Do you remember his exact words?"

"He said the inspectors had found some things that didn't correspond to the allocation contract."

"Was it a big job?"

"Yes. Constructing a low-income housing complex."

"Do you have any explanation for it?"

"No, sir. But I do know something strange."

"And what's that?"

"That exactly the same thing happened at the Spampinato building site in Montereale."

"So the inspectors never came to Montereale, either, and the site was shut down just the same?"

"That's exactly right. And so I got curious and asked around a little. You want to know what I found?"

"Of course."

"The inspectors went to only two building sites, Rosaspina's and Lo Schiavo's. They never showed their faces at the others."

"I was told, by a well-informed person, that they also went to the Albachiara site."

"No, sir, they didn't, I assure you. They want people to think that, but it's not true."

All at once a sort of lightbulb came on in the inspector's head and went out again just as fast.

"Were all the people working at your Farullo site legitimate?"

'Ntonio Garzullo suddenly went from being calm to squirming uncomfortably in his chair.

"What do you mean?"

"You know perfectly well what I mean."

The thunderclaps were making such a loud, constant rumble that they had to raise their voices to speak.

'Ntonio answered reluctantly, through clenched teeth. "Let's just say . . . about sixty per cent. The others don't have their papers in order. They're illegals, with no visas, no nothing . . . But, Jesus, Inspector, please . . ."

"You needn't worry."

"Anyway . . . They're not the only ones like that . . . It's the same at all the other building sites as well."

"Are the illegal workers paid under the table?"

"Yes, sir."

And how are those with their papers in order paid?"

"I don't understand the question."

"Are they paid by cheque? Wire transfer to a bank account? Cash?"

"They're paid in cash. Nobody makes it to a thousand euros a week anyway."

The lightbulb flashed on and off again in the inspector's brain.

He asked himself a precise question: and what if everyone, papers or not, was paid under the table?

Wouldn't that be a brilliant way to launder dirty money? He smiled at 'Ntonio, thanked him, and said goodbye.

As soon as he was alone, he rang Pasqualino, Adelina's son, who was a thief that the inspector had arrested in the past. Still, when he could, Pasqualino would do him a favour or two.

"What can I do for you, Inspector?"

"Are you busy right now?"

"Nah."

"I'd like to talk to you."

"I'm in the neighbourhood. I'll be right over."

He showed up about ten minutes later, took off his dripping raincoat, and sat down.

"I need some information," the inspector began.

"Here I am."

"Have you by any chance heard any talk about a really big theft that occurred a few days ago?"

"What was stolen?"

"Money. Which had been kept in a safe."

"A bank safe?"

"No, a private one."

"Here in Vigàta?"

"Yes. In the Pizzutello district."

"Where that young guy got killed?"

"Exactly."

Pasqualino shook his head.

"That's nothing to do with us. And I don't think it was anyone from the outside, either, or we woulda heard about it." And this was confirmation that the robbery hadn't involved common thieves, as Mimì had maintained.

As soon as Pasqualino went out, Augello came in.

"I've been racking my brains trying to remember where I saw that tattoo of the sun . . . Didn't this Pitrineddru give you any other details?"

"Everything he said to me I've already told you."

"If he could just tell me whether the man was bald, or what colour his hair was, or if he saw any scars . . ."

"I don't think he remembers. Aside from the fact that he's a big ape with the brains of a little kid, he must have been pretty upset by the scene he was witnessing."

"Think if I went and talked to him he'd start thumping me?"

"He might. But if you were able to identify this man, it would be a giant step forward for us."

"I know. That's why I've been tormenting myself."

"We could go there together. Me, he trusts. But I would have to tell him some kind of lie, like that Inge called and asked about him, and I don't feel like doing that. I feel sorry for him."

"Listen, I have an idea. What if I went to see him alone and told him I was a friend of Inge's who's just arrived from Germany and has greetings for him from her?"

"That might work."

"Then tell me how I should go about it."

"But do you want to go out there in this weather?"

"If I don't, I won't get any sleep tonight."

Montalbano even went so far as to draw him a sketch of the road and the footpath that led behind Pitrineddru's house, advising him strongly to avoid the old lady and to go at dusk.

At around half-past five he got a call from Gambardella, who sounded pleased.

"My dear Inspector, so sorry to trouble you."

"No trouble at all."

"I'm sorry, I didn't hear what you said. It sounds like Niagara Falls outside."

"I said, no trouble at all."

"I wanted to tell you that Asciolla called me. Apparently my little trick of the lost letter worked."

"What did he tell you?"

"He said that he was called in this morning by Riggio, the works manager, the man he'd argued with, who informed him that if he wanted to come back to work at Albachiara after the stoppage was lifted, it would be no problem."

"And what did Asciolla say?"

"He thanked him, pretended he was touched, and accepted the offer. He feels more reassured now and will call me back in a few days. What do you think?"

If the journalist was expecting the inspector to congratulate him, he was disappointed.

"Be very careful," said Montalbano.

"Careful about what?"

"This overnight change of heart on the part of Albachiara . . . rings false to me."

"Well, I'm convinced they've taken the bait. And that in so doing, they expect to secure Asciolla's silence."

"Whatever the case, I advise caution."

"I wasn't born yesterday," Gambardella said defensively.

"And do me a favour. If you should meet Asciolla, let me know in advance the time and place of the meeting."

He'd just put the receiver down when all the lights at the station went out.

The storm was at its peak, the wind was rattling the windowpanes, and the continual flashes of lightning lit everything up like daylight. Then a sort of comical interlude occurred. Catarella appeared in the doorway with a candle in his hand and a saucer in the other. But both his hands were shaking.

"I brung yiz a can'le."

"Why are you trembling?"

"'Cuz I'm ascared o' lightnings."

He tried to put the saucer down on the desk, but he was trembling so badly that it slipped out of his hands and fell to the floor.

When he bent down to pick it up, he put the candle down on all the papers still waiting to be signed, immediately setting them on fire.

Cursing the saints, Montalbano swatted at the pile, and the burning pages fell partly on the floor, and partly on Catarella, who was getting up again.

"Halp! Halp! I'm on fire!" Catarella yelled, running out of the room.

Bedlam broke out. Two officers rushed into the room and stamped out the fire.

"Go and see where Catarella's gone," the inspector ordered them.

At that moment the light returned, and Catarella with it. He was completely drenched, but proud.

"Ya know, Chief, soon as I catched fire, I tought it were best if I ran ousside inna rain to put ou' the fire. Wuz I right?"

CHAPTER
THIRTEEN

It was still raining buckets when he stepped into his house, even though the worst seemed almost over.

He decided to eat his dinner in the kitchen, since there was no question, with the powerfully gusting wind outside, of opening the French windows to the veranda.

The sea had covered the beach, taken it over, made it disappear. Another few feet and it would be crashing against the walls of the house.

He more than made up for his sparse midday meal by savouring, one bite at a time, the fantastic seafood salad and swordfish *involtini* Adelina had prepared for him.

Then he cleared the table and rang Livia.

"It's been raining very hard here, too, ever since this morning. But I had to go out anyway."

"Why?"

"Selene was being naughty. I guess she got tired of being cooped up at home. I took advantage of a break in the weather and . . ."

She broke off and sneezed.

"You see?" Montalbano said, irritated. "You really shouldn't be so careless, Livia, you haven't really fully recovered yet, and it would take very little to . . . You have to take care . . ."

"Are you lecturing me now? Over a common cold? Is this some kind of joke?"

So much the better. How nice it was to surrender to a combative Livia! Thank you, Selene, blessed be thy name.

Afterwards he sat down in his armchair and turned on the TV to watch the Free Channel's news report:

> . . . the collapse of one wing of Building B occurred around seven-thirty p.m., at the height of a violent storm. The complex's security guard, Augusto Pillitteri, fifty-six, who by chance was present when it happened, sustained injuries to the head and chest. He was taken to the Sant'Antonio Hospital of Montelusa and is on the danger list. A few months ago another building in the same school complex in Villaseta . . .

On hearing these last words, Montalbano sat up in his chair and listened very carefully.

> . . . was declared unfit for use shortly after it was turned over to the municipal government. We asked the engineer Emanuele Riggio, site superintendent of the complex for Albachiara Construction, for an explanation, which he was courteous enough to provide. Here is what he said.

169

Zito's face vanished and Riggio's appeared. He was a fiftyish man with rather drawn features, hair cut down almost to nothing, cold eyes, and a little gash in place of a mouth.

There is very little to explain. The entire complex sits on a site chosen not by us, mind you, but by the municipal governments of Vigàta and Montelusa, where the land is subject to dangerous movement. Naturally, before beginning work our company sought the opinion of the distinguished Professor Augusto Maraventano, who declared the area perfectly suitable for construction. After one building was declared unfit for use, the court ordered a further geological study, which unfortunately found inexplicable errors in the evaluation made by Professor Maraventano. For this reason, Albachiara has been cleared of all responsibility. Today's collapse must therefore be attributed solely and exclusively to the violent storm which, because of seepage, caused the ground to further give way.

The engineer's hard face, which had hardened even more while uttering the last sentence, disappeared, and Zito's reappeared.

This storm has caused other damage as well in several towns around the province. In Montelusa —

Montalbano turned it off.

170

He got up and started pacing about the room.

Though the engineer was playing it safe, the collapse was sure to revive and fan the gossip and insinuations that had arisen the previous time, when the first building had suffered damage.

Albachiara was sure to find itself again at the centre of suspicions and doubts at a rather delicate moment, since its Riguccio site had already been shut down because of irregularities.

And this all meant that an article from Gambardella based on Asciolla's revelations might deal a mortal blow to the firm and even send a few people to gaol.

Now, if the Albachiara people had no qualms about shooting a poor bricklayer who knew next to nothing about the firm's shady dealings, imagine what they might do to Asciolla, who knew quite a few things about them.

Enough to ruin them for ever.

He went to bed feeling worried for the journalist and the building site foreman.

They had to be more than cautious. Could they?

By the time he was asleep the wind had died down, but the rain was still falling.

He woke up later than usual.

It was still raining, and although it was eight o'clock, he could barely see indoors. There was a power cut. It was an hour before he was ready to leave.

The rough track that led from his house to the main road to Vigàta had turned into a torrent of mud. The inspector's car had trouble making it up the hill. The

Vigàta road was jammed with an interminable queue of stationary cars, bumper to bumper. It took him well over an hour to get to the station.

"Ah, Chief! Inna waitancy room 'ere'd be a lawyer called Cahoney wit' 'is client, an' 'ey wanna talk t'yiz poissonally in poisson."

"Cat, what kind of nonsense are you telling me?"

"Whassat, Chief?"

"That couldn't possibly be the lawyer's name."

"It seemed a li'l strange to me, too, Chief, bu' I swear onna stack o' Bybers, iss true."

"Fazio here?"

"Yeah, 'e's onna premisses."

"Send me Fazio first and then the lawyer."

"Got any news?" he asked Fazio as soon as he walked in.

"Yes."

"You can tell me later. For now, have a seat and let's listen to a lawyer who's come to talk to us."

There was a faint knock at the door.

"Come in!" the inspector said, standing up.

In came a tall, distinguished man of about forty-five, with a cordial smile and a relaxed manner. In his left hand he held an elegant briefcase that must have cost him a whole portfolio of stocks.

"Hello, my name is Eugenio Mahoney, barrister." He exchanged handshakes with Montalbano and Fazio. "And this is my client, Pino Pennisi."

Who held out his hand to no one, but only stood there with his arms dangling at his sides, eyes downcast and knees slightly bent.

172

"Please sit down," said Montalbano, indicating the two chairs opposite his desk.

Fazio, who'd remained standing, quickly wrote something on a piece of paper and handed it to the inspector.

"Here's that phone number you asked me for," he said, sitting down on the settee.

On the piece of paper were the words:

Pen brought Ing to Vig.

Montalbano remembered what Terrazzano had told him.

Inge had left Germany to come to Vigàta because she was engaged to a bricklayer here. This same Pino Pennisi who was now sitting in front of him.

"What can I do for you?" the inspector asked cordially.

The lawyer's friendly smile suddenly disappeared, and his face turned very serious.

"My client, Giuseppe Pennisi, known as Pino, has come to turn himself in," he said solemnly.

But it was as if he'd merely said that it was raining outside. Fazio remained impassive. Montalbano, for his part, seemed to lend no weight to these words.

He opened a drawer, riffled around for something inside, didn't find it, closed the drawer, then asked Fazio:

"Have you got a sweet?"

"No, sir, I'm sorry."

Montalbano then felt obliged to explain to the lawyer, who looked at him in bewilderment:

"Sometimes I get this itch in my throat, and only sweets . . . I'm sorry, you were saying your client has come to turn himself in?"

"Yes," said the lawyer.

He was drooping a little now. The business of the sweets had ruined the effect he'd hoped to create.

"What did he do?"

"He killed Gerlando Nicotra, in self-defence."

Montalbano and Fazio exchanged a glance and understood each other.

Act three had begun.

"Ah," the inspector said.

And that was all. Silence fell. Montalbano seemed to lose himself watching the raindrops pattering against the windowpanes, hurled by the gusting wind.

At last he spoke.

"If only I had a sweet . . ."

"Want me to go and look for one?" Fazio suggested, standing up.

"Yeah, would you?"

Fazio went out. Montalbano went *ahem, ahem* twice, stood up, went over to the window, went *ahem, ahem* twice again, then sat back down. The lawyer was watching his movements with stupefaction.

Fazio returned, placed a sweet on the desk, and sat down. The inspector unwrapped it and put it in his mouth with visible satisfaction.

"Ah," he said, "I feel better already."

"Do you want to hear how it happened?" the lawyer asked, wanting to retake control of the situation.

"Sure, why not?" said Montalbano.

"My client —" Mahoney began.

"I'd like to hear Mr Pennisi tell the story."

Pennisi gulped twice before beginning to speak. Then he opened his mouth and immediately closed it again, as though he suddenly lacked the strength.

"Come on, don't be shy," the lawyer said to him.

"From the beginning?" he asked.

"Yes."

He heaved a long sigh and began.

"I met Inghi when I was workin' as a bricklayer in Germany. She was about to turn twenty at the time. We fell in love and moved in together. She din' have no father or mother. 'Bout a year later I foun' out there was work down here an' so I decided to come back, an' Inghi came with me. We moved into a house with one o' my mother's sisters, and Inghi started workin' as a checkout girl in a supermarket. Six months later, one day I come home from work an' she's not there. My aunt said she came by in the afternoon, packed a suitcase in a hurry, and went away with a man who was waitin' for her in his car. After that, I di'n't see her again for a few years."

"Wait a second," the inspector interrupted him. "Are you telling me you immediately accepted the situation? Didn't you try to find her and bring her home?"

"Nossir."

"Weren't you even curious to know the name of the man she ran off with?"

"I already knew his name. It was Gaetano Pasanisi, the owner of the supermarket."

"How did you find out?"

"Inghi tol' me he was always chasin' after her and giving her presents and propositionin' her. And since she used to complain about me not bringin' home enough money, I 'mmediately realized who the man was she ran away with, and that there was no point in goin' lookin' for her."

"So you confirm that you hadn't seen each other again for all these years, not even by chance?"

"Yessir. Also 'cause she wasn't a checkout girl any more at the supermarket. She was a kept woman."

"Go on."

"Then, two months ago, since I work at the Rosaspina site in Pizzutello, one morning, I's on my way there when I saw her right in front of me, looking at me an' smilin'. I just kept on goin' but then she called me, so we talked a little, an' then she got on her bike and rode off."

"Do you remember what you said to each other?"

"She did most of the talkin'. She said she was married to Nicotra, the accountant, but they didn't have any kids, an' she showed me where she lived, right by the building site. She wanted to know if I was married, an' so I told her I was and that I had two kids."

"Did you know Nicotra?"

"I knew who he was. I sometimes seen him go by in his car, but I didn't know he was married to Inghi."

"And how did you say goodbye?"

176

Pennisi looked confusedly at the lawyer, then the inspector.

"What's 'at mean?"

"I just want to know whether, when you said goodbye to her, did you shake hands, did you embrace, or did you not do anything like that?"

Pennisi looked again at his lawyer; he seemed distressed.

"Tell him everything," said Mahoney.

"She . . . hugged me."

"And what did you do?"

"I hugged her, too."

"Did you kiss?"

"Nossir."

"Do you remember what time it was?"

"It was probably 'round eight-thirty in the morning. I was gettin' into work a little late."

"And this happened on the road leading to the building site?"

"Yessir."

"Wasn't there the risk someone might see the two of you?"

"Sure there was, but I don't think no one saw us."

"Go on."

"'Bout a week later, when I'd just turned onto the road to the site —"

"Were you in your car?"

"No, I was on my moped. Then a week later the same thing happened. She asked me if I wanted to come an' see her after work, 'cause she felt like talkin' about old times. She also said her husband wouldn't be back till eight, an' so we'd have a good hour or so. I said I was busy, but she insisted, an' so in the end I said OK."

"And you went to her house?"

"Yessir."

"Why?"

"I dunno."

"Were you in love with her again?"

"No, sir."

"Did you still desire her physically?"

"Yessir. An' maybe also because she still seemed taken with me, an' so I thought I could get revenge on her for leaving me."

"Did you sleep together?"

"Not that time, no."

"Tell me exactly what the two of you did."

"As soon as I got there, she said there was an uncle of hers from Germany stayin' in a room upstairs, but he wouldn't be comin' downstairs, an' so he wouldn't bother us."

"Wait a second. Did she ever talk to you about this uncle when you were together in Germany?"

"I don't think so."

"Go on."

"We sat down on the sofa an' she started talkin' to me an' holdin' my hand tight."

"What did she talk to you about?"

"She said she wasn't happy in her marriage, that her husband neglected her, that he'd made her so many promises but hadn't kept a single one, that it was better

178

when she was with me and worked as a checkout girl . . ."

"Did you kiss?"

"Yes."

"Did you make plans to meet again?"

"Yessir. She explained she wasn't always free between six an' eight, but she said I could definitely come back three days later. An' that time we made love."

"Where?"

"In the same big room downstairs where the sofa was."

"Tell me something. This uncle — did you ever hear him at least walking around upstairs?"

"Sure. But Inghi said he wouldn't come downstairs. An' in fact I never saw him once, not even by accident."

"Did you ever hear his voice?"

"Once, when he was talkin' on the phone."

"What was he speaking?"

Upon hearing the question, Pennisi's eyes opened wide, just like Pitrineddru's.

"What's that mean?"

The lawyer intervened.

"The inspector wants to know whether he was speaking Italian or German."

He'd stressed the last word.

"German," Pennisi said, echoing him.

"How many other times did you meet Inge before the time Nicotra caught you together?"

"Four times."

"Always between six and eight?"

"Yessir."

"Now tell me about that night."

"The last time, Inghi'd told me her husband said he had to go to Palermo after dinner the following evening, and he wouldn't be back until late the next morning. It was a good opportunity to finally spend a whole night together. So we planned for me to go there right after midnight, just to be safe. And before knocking, I was supposed to check whether the car was still in the garage. Which I did."

"What excuse did you give your wife?"

"I told her I was doin' some work on the side."

"At night? In the rain?"

"I made up a story about an internal wall in a house and said it was an emergency."

"And?"

"So I got there, saw that the car wasn't in the garage, and Inghi, who was waiting for me, let me inside. She told me to take off my shoes."

"Why?"

"First of all, because she didn't want me trackin' mud all over the house, and second, so I wouldn't make any noise comin' up the stairs. She was wearing slippers. So I took my shoes off, and she put them under the radiator at the other end of the room, so they could dry off. She did the same with my raincoat."

"So the two of you went upstairs to the bedroom?"

"Yessir, after Inghi turned off the light."

"Do you remember whether the door to her uncle's room was open or closed?"

"It was about three-quarters open."

180

"Was the light on?"

"No. I heard him snoring."

"And then?"

"Inghi led me into the bedroom and closed the door."

"Did she lock it?"

"No. Then I got undressed, she took off her dressing gown, and we got into bed. Outside the wind and the rain were just terrible."

"Did you have the light on?"

"No, sir. Inghi said . . . she said she liked to do it better in the dark with the lightning flashin'."

"When did Nicotra arrive?"

"Around three-thirty the wind and rain let up a little and we heard a car pull up and stop. Inghi recognized the sound of the engine. She started tremblin' and told me her husband was back. I found my clothes, went out of the room and into the uncle's room while Inghi remade the bed. Then she told me from behind the door to leave as soon as her husband fell asleep."

"Did you leave the uncle's door three-quarters open?"

"Yeah, and in fact I had trouble puttin' my clothes back on."

CHAPTER
FOURTEEN

At this point Pennisi stopped, opened his mouth and closed it again, and started squirming in his chair. His lawyer, who hadn't expected this interruption, looked at him with concern.

"What's wrong?" he asked.

Pennisi kept opening and closing his mouth as if he couldn't breathe. Then he murmured:

"I can't talk no more."

"Why not? What's come over you?" Mahoney asked, seeming more and more worried.

"My mouth is dry."

The lawyer's face brightened at once.

Montalbano wanted to laugh. Mahoney had been scared to death that Pennisi had either forgotten his lines or no longer felt like continuing.

Then Fazio, on the inspector's cue, stood up, filled a glass from the bottle of water that was always on top of the filing cabinet, and handed it to Pennisi.

The young man drank it down in a single gulp.

"Do you want to continue, or would you rather wait and resume after a break?" Montalbano asked.

"Let's continue, let's continue," said the lawyer.

"Let him decide," said the inspector.

Pennisi nodded. But since Montalbano said nothing, Mahoney tried to get things going again.

"My client is ready to —"

"Yeah, I got that. How long did it take Nicotra to put the car in the garage and then come upstairs?"

"I don't remember."

"Try."

"I dunno, six, seven minutes. In the meantime I put my clothes back on and was right behind the door."

"Afraid?"

"Who?"

"What do you mean, 'who'? You. Were you afraid?"

"Of course."

"Were you sweating?"

"I don't —"

"Trembling?"

"I said I don't —"

"Was your throat all dry like a minute ago?"

"*Matre santa!* I —"

"I don't see the point of these questions," Mahoney interrupted nervously.

"You surprise me, counsel! Are you going to claim self-defence or not?"

"Of course I am!"

"Well, my questions were aimed at trying to understand what state of mind your client was in. But if you don't . . . I'll desist, you know."

"No, no, of course not . . ."

"OK, let's drop that subject. Once he was upstairs, what did Nicotra do?"

"He asked Inghi if she was asleep, and she didn't answer. So he went into the bathroom and stayed in there a really long time."

"How long?"

Pennisi looked at him as though completely bewildered. He was all sweaty and his hands were shaking. "What do you mean?"

"Can't you be a little more precise? 'A really long time' is a little vague, don't you think?"

Thrown by this, Pennisi turned to the lawyer. "How long was he in there?" he asked him.

"How should I know?" Mahoney said, irritated.

"Shall we say fifteen minutes?" the inspector suggested.

"All right."

"Then what happened?"

"When he went back into the bedroom, it was past four o'clock. A little while later he got up, muttering to himself, and went downstairs, maybe to drink some water. Then finally, about half an hour later, I realized he'd fallen asleep."

"How could you tell?"

"His breathing was regular."

"Didn't you suspect he might be faking it?"

"Nossir."

"In your opinion, how did Nicotra come to realize that there was a stranger in the house? Did he see your raincoat and shoes in the room downstairs?"

"I don't think he saw them."

"Why do you say that?"

"Because they were at the back of the room, in the sitting area, and the light was off over there."

"And so?"

"In my opinion, the story about him havin' to go to Palermo wasn't true. He just made it up. It was a trap, and me and Inghi fell right into it. If anything, he knew I was there when he saw my moped parked by the garage."

"But that doesn't explain how Nicotra found out that his wife was cheating on him with you."

"Maybe somebody told him."

"Who?"

"Maybe a friend of mine who saw me going to see Inghi."

"What reason would this person have had for making trouble for you?"

"I dunno, maybe he was jealous . . . that I was . . . Inghi . . . is a fine-lookin' girl, you know."

"Tell me what you did when you thought Nicotra had fallen asleep."

"I started moving very carefully."

"Meaning?"

"I went out of the room."

"And the uncle never woke up?"

"No."

"How strange!" said the inspector.

"The man may be hard of hearing, or perhaps he took sleeping pills," said the lawyer.

"Yes, of course . . . And after you left the room?"

"I'm sure it took me fifteen minutes to go down the stairs, that's how slow I was goin'."

"And when you got downstairs, what did you do?"

"I was so confused an' scared that the only thing I could think of was to get out of that house, an' so I went an' opened the door, which was only closed with the spring lock. So I opened it but then I realized I was barefoot. So I ran to the far end of the room, put on my shoes, which were under the radiator, grabbed my raincoat, and went back over to the door, but then Nicotra's voice stopped me in my tracks."

"What did he say?"

"Stop or I'll shoot."

"Did he shout it?"

"I don't think so."

"Did he whisper it?"

"I dunno, I just heard it, that's all."

"So you froze and . . .?"

"I instinctively put my hands up an' heard him say, as he's walkin' up to me, that he wanted to have a good look at the man who was fuckin' his wife."

"So not for a second did he take you for a burglar?"

"Nossir."

"Then what?"

"I realized I was screwed. When he was right next to me, he told me to turn around. Without thinking twice, since I was already done for, I turned around really fast and threw the raincoat I was holding in my raised right hand in his face and —"

"My compliments. Good move," Montalbano commented.

Then, turning to Fazio: "Don't you think it was a good move?"

"An excellent move," Fazio said, continuing to write as he'd been doing for a while, since the inspector had signalled him to do so when he'd returned to the room.

"And then?"

"And then I grabbed his hand and tried to wrestle the gun away from him, but I couldn't. He kneed me in the balls but I didn't let go, despite the pain. Then as we was still strugglin' and both almost outside the door, he suddenly had his back to me but the arm that was holdin' the gun was turned towards me to my advantage. So I twisted his hand until he had to let go, and then I disarmed him, pushed him away, and shot him, all at the same time. I didn't mean to — it was just a kind of instinctive reaction."

"The natural instinct of self-preservation," Mahoney emphasized.

"Go on, go on," Montalbano said enthusiastically.

"After the shot, I just stood there in shock. I saw him grab Inghi's bike, which was just outside the door, and ride off. At this point Inghi, who'd come downstairs and witnessed part of our struggle, kinda went crazy."

"What did she say?"

"She started screamin' and holdin' me really tight and trembling all over, and sayin' they would blame it on her and I couldn't just leave her like that. Then she ran upstairs and called her uncle."

"And he'd remained upstairs all this time?"

"Yessir."

"Don't you think it's strange he didn't come down even when he heard the shot?"

"Maybe he was afraid."

"Go on."

"I took advantage of the situation to run and grab my moped and get out of there as fast as I could."

"Did you go in the same direction as Nicotra?"

"That's the only way out of there."

"Did you catch him up?"

"Nossir. I didn't even see him."

"I get the impression that you never saw Inge again after that."

"That's right."

"Listen, what did you do with that pistol? It was a pistol, right, not a revolver?"

"Yes, an Italian pistol, a Beretta. A friend o' mine had one just like it. I found it in my pocket as I was going home. I didn't even remember putting it there."

"Do you still have it?"

"No, I threw it off the bridge over the Simeto, which by then was more mud than water."

"One last thing I'm curious about. We found the pillow on the uncle's bed covered with blood. Did you strike him that night, perhaps to keep him quiet?"

"Nossir. But Inghi did tell me once about that problem."

"What problem?"

"One day she told me that sometimes her uncle suddenly starts bleedin' from the nose."

"Ah, so that's it!" the inspector exclaimed. "So, the following day, did you go and check to see whether Inge was still in the house or had gone away?"

"No, sir, I didn't."

188

"Did you know that we found Nicotra's car burnt out?"

"Yessir, I saw it on TV."

"But you have no explanation for it."

"Nossir."

"And there you have it," the lawyer said at this point. "Now, if you could just read the record back to us —"

"What record?" said the inspector, looking astonished.

"Why, the record of what my client has confessed . . . and which your assistant has been writing down . . ."

"Were you by any chance taking all this down?" Montalbano asked Fazio with an air of surprise.

"Me? No. You never told me to. I was just writing the memo you wanted."

"See? There's no record of the proceedings."

The lawyer completely lost his composure.

"But what fucking way of doing things is this?" he asked, raising his voice.

"Use decent language and lower your voice."

"What?! You spend half an hour taking my client's confession, and then —"

"I didn't *take* anything! Don't try to reshuffle the cards! You asked me if I wanted to listen to what had happened, and I, purely out of politeness, agreed to do so."

"But you're denying the obvious! You started asking all kinds of detailed questions!"

"Of course! Curiosity got the better of me. It's such a thrilling story!"

The lawyer bit his lip, adjusted his tie, and tried to calm himself down.

"Must I infer from your attitude that you refuse to begin arrest proceedings?"

"Are you joking? But please don't infer anything, I beg you! I have given due consideration to the situation and will proceed accordingly. Just sit tight for another five minutes, and I'll contact the proper authorities presently."

He dialled a number on the outside line and started speaking.

"Prosecutor Jacono? Good morning, sir. Sorry to trouble you, but a lawyer by the name of Mahoney has come to our station with his client, a certain Giuseppe Pennisi, who says he killed Gerlando Nicotra. What should I do? Ah, you want to talk to him right away? Yes, yes, OK."

He hung up.

"All taken care of. Prosecutor Jacono says he'll be waiting for you and your client. Would you like us to drive you there in one of our cars, or would you rather take your own?"

"We'll take mine. Good day," said the lawyer, face red with rage.

He grabbed Pennisi by the shoulder, after his client had sat back down in utter confusion, and dragged him out of the office.

Fazio couldn't help laughing.

"*Matre santa!* That lawyer was about to burst like a balloon! Our theatrics really got to him!"

Montalbano, on the other hand, was serious.

"What's wrong, you worried?" asked Fazio.

"No, but I was thinking that there must be some pretty subtle minds behind this whole affair. Who are thinking things through, down to the finest details. Take the story of Inge getting Pennisi to take his wet shoes off. You know why they made that up? Because they thought we might have heard, from the Forensics analyses, that there were no footprints from his shoes. And they also found a good explanation for the blood on the pillow. The uncle suffered from frequent nosebleeds. The uncle who spoke German. Hats off. But they're unaware of the three aces we're holding: Pitrineddru's testimony; the fact — unknown to them — that both the uncle and Nicotra were armed; and, finally, that we discovered the underground safe."

"So what happens now?"

"That depends."

"On what?"

"If Jacono has read Forensics' report, he'll be wondering where the Beretta came from when there were already two Russian revolvers in the house, and he'll start putting the screws on Pennisi. If he hasn't read it, he'll arrest him."

"But can you explain to me why you won't just go to Jacono and tell him exactly how things stand?"

"Because the more they believe we've swallowed their bait, the better. And now let's talk about what I'm interested in. Did you get all the names?"

"Yes. I've got the names of the heads of all six companies."

He took a sheet of paper out of his jacket pocket. Montalbano stopped him.

"I'm not interested in knowing them. Now listen up. First of all, I want to know whether any of them is in any way related, closely or remotely, by blood or marriage, to either the Sinagras or the Cuffaros. And if there are no blood relations, I want to know whether at any time in the past there have been other kinds of relations: friendship, business, godfathers, godmothers, and so on . . . Got that?"

"Got it."

"Afterwards, you must do another very important thing. Before being taken on at Rosaspina, did Nicotra, when he was still working for Primavera, have any assistant accountants working under him? And if so, where do these people work now?"

Augello came in.

"Good morning to all. I have a cold."

"How much time do I have?" Fazio asked the inspector.

"Two days."

Fazio got up and shot out of the room.

"Want to know the big news of the day? Nicotra's killer came here to turn himself in."

"Really?" Mimì asked, astonished.

"It's a nice little tale of adultery you're sure to like. Have a seat and I'll tell you the whole story. And then I'll explain why it's all a sham."

"I wonder what mountain-high pile of shit they're trying to cover up?" Augello asked when the inspector had finished.

"I'm starting to get an idea."

"Let me in on it."

"It's still too early to talk about it. What about you? Did you meet Pitrinnedru?"

"Forget about me. All I got out of it was this cold."

"But did you talk to him?"

Augello grimaced.

"When I got there it was pouring, and I had to take the little road that leads behind the house on foot, getting drenched in the process. Pitrineddru was in the chicken coop, under the roof. I called to him and he came out and approached me. 'Who are you?' he asked me. I wanted to reply that I was a friend of Inge's but I was only able to get out the words 'I am' before he punched me right in the stomach, saying, 'You're a stupid policeman, 'a'ss what you are.' And he went back into the chicken coop."

"So what did you do?"

"What was I supposed to do, in your opinion, with a gorilla that size? Arrest him? Shoot him? I got back in my car and drove back here. A lot of effort for nothing."

"So you still can't remember where you saw the man with the tattoo?"

"Utter darkness."

He got to the trattoria so late that Enzo had already started clearing the tables.

"Is there anything left for me?" the inspector asked.

"I'll put some pasta on to boil immediately."

"No, never mind. No first course. Just bring me a large helping of seafood antipasto."

"Yes, sir. And would you like a dish of sea bass after that?"

"Sounds perfect."

But Enzo didn't move.

"What's up?"

"I beg your pardon, but is it true that the man who killed Nicotra gave himself up?"

"Yes, it's true. But how did you find out?"

"I heard it on television, on Tele Vigàta."

"When?"

"This morning, on the eleven o'clock report."

How was that possible?

At eleven Pennisi and his lawyer were at the police station, and therefore nobody, theoretically, was in any position to know anything yet. And so it was clear that the information broadcast on Tele Vigàta had been passed over by the author of the comedy, so that it would immediately become public knowledge.

But why the hurry?

The answer was simple. To have the case closed as quickly as possible in order to block further investigation.

Montalbano had just finished his sea bass when Enzo came over to tell him he was wanted on the phone.

"Beckin' yer partin' fer the distoibancy while y'er eatin', Chief, but —"

"What is it, Cat?"

"Prossecator Giacono called askin' if you could partake yerself onna premisses o' his office, him bein' him, Prossecator Giacono, at tree-toity."

The inspector looked at his watch. He had just enough time.

CHAPTER
FIFTEEN

"I had no choice but to put Pennisi behind bars," was the first thing Jacono said as he was showing Montalbano in. "But I haven't yet made up my mind to request confirmation of the arrest."

"Why?"

"That's exactly why I summoned you here. So we could discuss this affair in peace. I confess the whole thing has got me a little perplexed."

"I'm at your service," said the inspector. "But could I read the transcript first?"

"Here you go," said Jacono, handing it to him. Montalbano scanned it.

It corresponded word for word with what Pennisi had said at the station.

He gave it back to Jacono.

"What is it you find unconvincing?" asked Montalbano.

"Well . . . First of all, there's this general impression that the whole thing was . . . well, forced . . . I'll try to explain. Did you suspect Pennisi in any way? Had you started investigating him?"

"It was the furthest thing from my mind."

"So he didn't feel hunted. Therefore, since he never once gave any sign of feeling remorse for what he'd done, why did he feel the need to turn himself in? If he hadn't, his name would have never even come up."

"Anything else?"

"Yes. For example, the murder weapon — by Pennisi's account — was a Beretta pistol. Since I knew from the Forensics report that Nicotra kept a large and perfectly well-functioning revolver in his bedside table, I asked Pennisi if he was really sure that it was a Beretta. And he said he was absolutely certain. So my question is: where did this weapon come from?"

"There's an easy answer to that question. It was kept in a safe in the Rosaspina offices, according to what Nino Barbera, the lawyer, told me of his own accord. He's on the firm's board of directors. And Nicotra pilfered it."

"But that's not the least bit logical!" Jacono snapped. "To go and steal a gun to shoot your wife's lover when you have a revolver already within reach!"

"Indeed. And that's not the only inconsistency, mind you. There are two other huge ones in Pennisi's story that cast doubt on whether he'd ever even set foot in that house."

"Tell me."

"The first is that Pennisi claimed that as soon as he entered Inge's house she made him take off his wet, muddy shoes and then went and put them on the floor under the radiator to help them dry. Forensics, who carefully checked the floor in that room, did find footprints from the muddy shoes of two people, but never found any trace of mud under the radiator. And yet, if the shoes had been put on the floor all messy and wet, they should have left some trace."

"Quite correct. Please continue."

"The second is a huge, almost ridiculous oversight, like the story of the gun. Pennisi told us that when he heard Nicotra come home unexpectedly, he grabbed his clothes and ran into the uncle's bedroom, where the old man was sleeping like a rock, and hid behind the door, which was three-quarters open. Three-quarters, mind you. And he also said he had trouble putting his clothes back on because there wasn't enough room. The problem is, none of this is remotely possible."

"Why not?"

"Because the door to the uncle's room, like all the doors on that floor, open outwards and not into the rooms. Therefore Pennisi would inevitably have already been spotted by Nicotra once he'd reached the top of the stairs. In order to hide, if anything he should not have gone into the room but remained in the hallway, behind the three-quarters-open door."

Jacono remained silent for a moment, with a faraway look in his eyes, not focusing on anything. Then he asked:

"What do you think, personally?"

"Have you read the Forensics report on the underground safe we discovered?"

"Yes."

"I think the crux of the whole story is in fact the safe and the millions of euros inside."

"I'm beginning to think the same thing."

"So they're going to try and throw us off the scent, to lead us away from something not big, but enormous. Luckily, however, they don't know, and for the moment they absolutely must not find out, that we discovered the safe. They also don't know — because they were never told — that both Nicotra and the so-called uncle were armed. These are two big cards to be played at the right moment."

Jacono's normally serious face became even more serious. "Let's get right to the point, I think it's best. You're suggesting to me indirectly that it would be more useful to the investigation if I were to pretend to believe Pennisi's self-accusation."

Montalbano didn't hesitate for a moment. "If you prefer, I'll suggest it to you directly."

Jacono absorbed the blow and then said: "What do you hope to gain?"

"Clearly the break-in at Nicotra's house and his consequent death have created serious problems for a certain group of people. And this group is trying to frame the occurrence as a case of marital infidelity that ended in tragedy. The picture they're holding up for us is this. I'll describe it for you, if you don't mind: the husband catches them by surprise, Pennisi disarms him and then kills him and runs away. Nicotra's wife, afraid the crime will be pinned on her, gets in her car and also runs away, taking her uncle with her. She gets back in touch from Germany, through a lawyer, using a commonplace excuse."

"That part I don't know," said Jacono.

Montalbano told him about it and then continued.

"If we make it seem that we believe all this and manage to convince them of it, they will feel more relaxed and will do something they can't do as long as the investigation is still ongoing."

"You say 'they'. But do you have any idea who 'they' are?"

"I'm starting to. And one of them has come out into the open."

"You mean the lawyer Barbera?"

"Exactly. Who sits on Rosaspina's board of directors, the company for which Nicotra was the chief accountant. And for whom our friend Pennisi works as a bricklayer. Bear in mind also that Nicotra went into a Rosaspina building site to die. Just a few yards more and he would have reached the main road, where he could have asked for help from some passing motorist. But he chose to turn off and let his body be found at the building site. In my opinion, he was trying to give us a very valuable clue."

"Let me get this straight. You think that Rosaspina is behind all this?"

"No, sir, I think Rosaspina is just one part of the whole."

Jacono didn't press him any further. He just paused thoughtfully again and then said:

"The only way open to us to get everyone to publicly believe we've taken the bait is to request the confirmation of the arrest. Which I'll do today."

"Thank you, sir."

As soon as he was outside, he had an idea and rang Zito at the Free Channel.

"Could you do a quick interview with me?"

"Do you want to talk about the Nicotra case?"

"Yes."

"I await you with open arms."

Fifteen minutes later he was in front of a TV camera, ready to go live for the afternoon broadcast, having gone over the questions with Zito.

"Inspector Montalbano, can you confirm the rumours that Pino Pennisi, a bricklayer, gave himself up for having killed the accountant Gerlando Nicotra?"

"I can and do confirm them. He gave a full, detailed confession to Prosecutor Jacono, who will request confirmation of his arrest by the end of the day."

"Can you tell us the motive?"

"Pennisi had been the lover of Nicotra's wife, Inge Schneider, for some time. Nicotra caught them in the act and threatened to kill Pennisi, but Pennisi was able to disarm him and then shot him in reaction."

"Where is Inge Schneider at present?"

"In Germany. She fled there after the crime, worried that she would be held responsible, taking with her her uncle, who had been a guest in her house for several months."

"But how do you explain the fact that the car that Inge escaped in was found burnt out?"

"Naturally, Pennisi could tell us nothing about this. It is my opinion that after Inge made her decision to

return to Germany, she set fire to her car herself, in a naive attempt to throw us off the trail."

"Can we therefore consider the case closed?"

"*That is my conviction."*

He went back to Vigàta feeling pleased, his little task having gone quite well.

"Fazio here?"

"'E ain't onna premisses, Chief."

"Know where he went?"

"Nah, Chief."

"Get him on his mobile and put the call through to my office."

He sat down and the telephone rang.

"Where are you?"

"In Montelusa, Chief. I'm doing that research you asked me to do."

"There's another thing I want you to do at the same time."

"Tell me."

"I want to know how the workers at all the different building sites were paid."

"What do you mean?"

"How did they receive their payment? Bank transfer? Cheque? Cash? For one of the sites, I already know, but you go ahead and inform yourself about all six. And we'll meet again tomorrow morning."

As soon as he hung up, the outside line rang. It was Gambardella.

"Can I come by around nine?"

"I'll be waiting for you."

Catarella came in.

"Beckin' yer partin' an' all, Chief, but I got astracted an' forgot som'n."

"What'd you forget?"

"'At there's the *raggiunieri* Nicotira onna premisses, the father o' the dead corpus, an' 'e wants a talk t'yiz poissonally in poisson."

"OK."

Ragioniere 'Gnazio Nicotra, compared to the last time he came into the station, was a changed man. The grief over the death of his son had bent him in two, and he swayed a little as he walked, as though drunk.

Montalbano felt terribly sorry for him. He got up to meet him and pulled out a chair for him.

"Whatever I can do to help . . ."

"There's nothing in particular I need to ask of you. I came here to . . . I'm sorry, but I just want to talk to someone . . . I have nobody with whom I can get these things off my chest."

"You can talk to me."

"I just can't get over the fact that it was Pennisi himself who betrayed him and then killed him."

Pennisi himself? What could these words mean? But the inspector thought it best not to ask any questions.

"Pennisi," the old man began, "was the man who got engaged to Inge and brought her here, but then Inge left him because he was too dissolute; his addiction to gambling and prostitutes always left him penniless. So one day, after she was married to my son, Pennisi called her and begged her to help him. She talked to Giugiù

202

about it, and my son quickly got him hired at the building site of the firm where he was the accountant."

"Rosaspina?"

"No, before that. At the time, Giugiù worked in Sicudiana with Rosales's firm, Belgiorno, and when Rosales later set up Primavera, Giugiù had Pennisi come over with him, and then he did the same again when Primavera went bankrupt and Rosaspina took over. Rosales had a lot of faith in Giugiù; he considered him almost a son."

"How was that?"

"Rosales had only one child, Stefano, who'd been a friend of Giugiù's since elementary school. Not a day went by that my son didn't go to the Rosaleses' house. Then, when he was ten years old, Stefano was hit by a car and killed. For ever after that, Rosales had a special regard for Giugiù. Though now, poor Rosales, well, he is the way he is."

"I don't know anything about this Rosales. This is the first I've ever heard of him. What's wrong with him?"

"Emilio Rosales was a powerful entrepreneur who always conducted his business between Sicudiana and Trapani. The only time he won a government contract in our area with Primavera, things went bad for him, and he had to halt the work and shut it all down. He was put on trial and convicted, retired from business, and is currently ill and under house arrest in Sicudiana."

But Nicotra was interested mostly in talking about the ingratitude of humanity, of people like Pennisi who repaid kindness with treachery and murder.

And because of this Montalbano got home from work an hour later than usual.

It was almost eight-thirty when he walked through the front door. On his way to the kitchen to see what Adelina had prepared for him, he stopped in his tracks. He wasn't going to have time to eat properly, the way he liked; he would have to shovel in one forkful after another without being able to enjoy it. And so he decided to open neither the fridge nor the oven.

All he could do before Gambardella arrived was phone Livia.

He dialled her number.

"How are you?"

"A lot better, thanks. Selene keeps me busy, keeps the dark thoughts at bay, and . . . Listen, you haven't told me anything about yourself or your work for quite a long time . . ."

She was finally taking an interest in him again! His heart filled with contentment. He immediately complied.

"OK, I'll tell you something really unusual. This morning a man came to the station to give himself up for a murder he most certainly did not commit."

"Why would he do that? Maybe he was covering for someone he loved or a family member?"

"No, it has nothing to do with his family; he's trying to throw us off the trail by covering for a gang of crooks."

"Why give himself up for that?"

"Look, this person is a bricklayer who loves to gamble. They probably promised to pay off his debts and give him a large sum for his wife and children."

"But he'll go to gaol for years and years!"

"Are you so sure? Meanwhile they're claiming self-defence. Anyway, you know how these things usually go, don't you? The worst he'll get is five years, max, and then he'll be out and he won't need to look for work any more, either. It's a pretty good investment, don't you think?"

Livia didn't answer. Montalbano continued. "Unfortunately for him, however, that's not how it'll turn out. He'll go to gaol anyway, for having tried to obstruct the investigation. But he won't get a cent for his trouble."

"Poor guy," said Livia.

This irritated the inspector.

"What do you mean, 'poor guy'? He's just a —"

The doorbell rang.

"I'm sorry, Livia, someone I was waiting for has arrived. I have to go. Good night."

He went and opened the door, and Gambardella entered. Since it had started raining again, Montalbano sat him down in the usual chair.

"I hear the prosecutor has requested confirmation of Pennisi's arrest. So was it really a case of adultery?"

Montalbano hesitated for a moment. Could he tell him the truth or not?

He decided he could.

"Not at all. It's a well-planned attempt to throw us off, but it suits us very well, for the moment, to pretend it's real. Now tell me about yourself."

"I've established direct contact with Asciolla."

"Did you meet?"

"Yes."

"Where?"

"In an absolutely safe place. An abandoned quarry near Montelusa."

"Are you sure nobody saw you?"

"Quite sure."

"I beg your pardon, but you take things a little too easy. And you didn't keep to our agreement. I told you to let me know in advance —"

"I know. But it wasn't from neglect, believe me. I just didn't have the time."

"You're playing with fire, you know. Do you realize that?"

"But, Inspector —"

"After this second collapse, Albachiara are again vulnerable to all manner of criticism. They're going through a difficult moment and will defend themselves by all means possible, including murder. Is that clear? They've already given us a taste of this with Piscopo."

"I give you my word it won't happen again. Next time I'll let you know beforehand."

"OK, now talk."

"Asciolla told me the reasons he was sacked. His row, as site foreman, with the works manager, Riggio, revolved essentially around two points. The first was the quality of the materials being used, which were quite inferior to those stipulated in the contract. The second was that the finished product was notably different from the approved design."

"Different in what sense?"

"Asciolla cited a few examples for me, but I couldn't grasp much. He said that the load-bearing cement beams were simply placed on the walls, not tied into them, creating a grave risk of instability. Asciolla knew that it wouldn't take much to expose the defects, and he was worried that the whole thing would be blamed on them. Anyway, seeing that he got nowhere in his first meeting, he requested a second, which the engineer granted him, in his office, with no witnesses. And that was when they had the quarrel that led to his dismissal."

Montalbano grimaced.

"What's wrong?"

"What's wrong is that Asciolla has no evidence to prove what he says."

Gambardella smiled. "Asciolla's a clever man."

"Meaning?"

"For the second meeting he'd put a recorder in his pocket. And he recorded everything."

Montalbano started in his chair. "Really?"

"Really."

"Did he have it with him?"

"No. But he's agreed to let me hear it at our next meeting."

"I want to be there, too."

"I don't think Asciolla will accept that."

"Just try, anyway."

"I'll try to persuade him."

"And what will you do once you have the recording?"

"I'll take it to a notary and have a sworn transcription made."

"Then what?"

"Then I'll publish it."

"Why not turn it over to a public prosecutor?"

"Because he would steal my scoop."

"You must give me your word that you will talk to me first before publishing it."

"All right. You have my word."

"And now I would like some information from you."

"What do you want to know?"

"Have you ever heard of a man named Emilio Rosales?"

"Of course. Rosales, in my opinion, is one of the most intelligent, imaginative, even ingenious, I would say, and unscrupulous crooks who has ever operated on this island of ours."

CHAPTER
SIXTEEN

Montalbano looked at him in shock.

"Are you serious? I don't understand how I could never have heard of him."

"It's because he's always managed to remain in the shadows. He always gets off by the skin of his teeth. He's always been, or used to be, devilishly clever. He has some very powerful political friends. He hobnobs with high society, has been president of a few football teams and exclusive sports clubs . . . Bear in mind that the only time he came out into the open was for the trial against Primavera, the company he was president of . . . That whole business was handled by the carabinieri, and the trial was held in Trapani. Therefore —"

"I was told he's very ill and under house arrest in Sicudiana."

"You were misinformed. He's under no restrictions whatsoever."

"So he can move about as he pleases?"

"No, he's retired from business, and is housebound by his illness. They say he doesn't want to see anyone and receives no visitors."

For whatever reason, this character piqued the inspector's curiosity.

"Tell me more about him."

"I could go on for hours."

"Just give me a summary. Tell me only the things you think are essential."

"Rosales was the son of a Trapanese fisherman who, through great sacrifice, was able to put him through law school. A fine, handsome young man, he soon got his university girlfriend pregnant, who was also from Trapani and the sole heir to the large Bordinaro family fortune. The shotgun wedding brought Rosales a substantial dowry. Either due to his life of luxury, or to some speculation gone wrong, he was soon broke again. And so he founded an investment company, Bella Stagione, which promised can't-miss deals and fleeced a few hundred gullible souls. Rosales was tried and acquitted. It was his business partner, upon whom he'd managed, quite skilfully, to shift all the blame, who took the fall and got convicted. He then set up a cooperative, which he called the 21st of March, in order to exploit an imaginary gold lode in South Africa that turned out to be another huge scam. And it ended in incredible fashion. He went into court as a defendant, and came out as an injured party."

"Brilliant."

"Where was I? After that, according to gossip, he becomes the clean face, so to speak, of the local crime boss Aguglia, and gets involved in construction. And his company starts to get all the best government contracts. And even though he is accused repeatedly of corruption, suborning the competition, and suchlike, he always gets off scot-free. A few years ago, however, he made a mistake."

"What was that?"

"In hopes of expanding his sphere of activity, he boldly pushed his way into our area, invading turf that traditionally belongs to the Cuffaros and Sinagras."

"And winning the contract for the new water main?"

"I see you've understood perfectly. And Primavera's failure, leading to the arrest of Rosales and others, was nothing more than the result of the war that the Sinagras and Cuffaros had been waging on him."

After eating in the kitchen, he felt the need for some fresh air.

He went out onto the veranda. It was raining, but ever so lightly. The bench, however, was wet. So he brought a chair outside and set himself up with whisky and cigarettes. There was no need to turn on the light outside. The one in the dining room sufficed.

The sound of the waves not only didn't trouble his thoughts, it actually helped them form and then cradled them.

He thought of Rosales's failed company, called Primavera. Which called to mind Botticelli's *Primavera*.

And, after that, a very old song that went: "*È primavera, svegliatevi bambine . . .*"

Primavera meant "spring", and with spring came roses. Rosebud.

And what was this Rosebud?

Ah, yes, it was in that beautiful film by Orson Welles — what was the title? . . . Anybody's guess . . . the one where the dying millionaire says, "Rosebud," and no one ever works out that he wanted the little sledge he used to play with as a boy, which was called "Rosebud" . . .

How strange, this attachment people sometimes have to certain names . . . that they carry along with them their whole lives . . .

Like Rosales, for example, with Bella Stagione, 21st of March, Primavera . . .

Wait a second, Montalbà, wait just one second.

Weren't Rosaspina, Albachiara, and Soledoro also the kind of names Rosales would have liked?

Of course they were. What an idiotic idea.

If Rosales had already tried to challenge the Cuffaros and Sinagras with his Primavera site and lost everything, it was unlikely those three other building sites were his.

Still, those three names . . .

Rosaspina . . . Albachiara . . . Soledoro . . . No, there was no point in racking his brains.

All he could do, for the time being, was wait for the results of Fazio's search.

He went to bed, but slept poorly.

At seven the next morning he was drinking a large cup of espresso when the telephone rang.

"Is this Inspector Montalbano?" asked a voice he did not recognize at first.

"Yes. Who . . . ?"

"I got your number from your office. I'm sorry to bother you at home. This is Jacono."

The prosecutor? What could he want at that time of day?

"What is it?"

"I was just informed by the prison management that a fight broke out in the showers this morning . . . Pennisi was involved and . . . well, he died from three stab wounds."

It was a powerful blow, and so sudden that it left the inspector speechless.

"I'm going over there now to see what happened, but I wanted to let you know as soon as possible. I'll keep you informed."

"Th . . . thank you," Montalbano stuttered. And yet he should have expected as much.

Surely it was not a chance tussle that broke out in the showers. It had been ordered from the outside, for the sole purpose of killing Pennisi.

Now, with him gone, it would be impossible to contest the lies he'd told.

And his little performance, now sealed once and for all by death, would take on the appearance of the truth.

They'd just scored a huge point in their favour. It was going to be hard to overcome the disadvantage.

But the inspector didn't feel disheartened. On the contrary.

He felt a rage rising up inside him that hadn't been there before, a silent, heavy rage that he would have to keep under control to avoid wrecking things, but which was roaring inside him like an engine at full throttle struggling to burst free of the brakes.

He was sipping the last of the coffee when somebody rang the doorbell.

And who could that be?

Curiosity aroused, he went to the door and found Gambardella standing in front of him.

A Gambardella who apparently had got dressed in a hurry, with half his shirt dangling out of his trousers, no tie, hair uncombed, and terror in his eyes.

He came in without saying hello and without asking permission, and went and sat in the armchair.

"What's going on?"

"Half an hour ago I got a phone call from Asciolla. He sounded terrified. He's left Vigàta with his family but didn't want to tell me where he was calling from."

"Try to calm down and tell me everything in order."

"Could I have some water?"

Montalbano went and got him some.

"He told me in essence that he was dropping everything and that he'd destroyed the recording."

"Why on earth?!"

"Well, from what I was able to gather, yesterday evening, right after dinner, Asciolla's daughter, Anita, went out to go to a friend's house to do her homework. Her friend lives about a ten-minute walk away. Then, about half an hour after she'd left the house, her friend called, asking why she hadn't arrived. Asciolla had barely put the receiver down when there was another call. A man's voice said he had Anita, and that he and his friends were going to have a little fun with her and then send her home. If he called the police they would kill her. And he ended by saying that it would be better for everyone if Asciolla had a change of scene as soon as his daughter got back. Two hours later, Anita returned in an awful state. Luckily, they hadn't done anything to her. Two men had seized her and kept her bound and gagged in a van. Asciolla took their advice, packed his bags, and fled."

"Apparently they saw you when you met Asciolla at the quarry, and they immediately sprang into action. I'd warned you."

Gambardella threw up his hands in resignation. The inspector twisted the knife in the wound.

"And now I just got a call telling me that Pennisi was murdered in gaol."

Gambardella's eyes opened wide.

"One way or another, they've made a clean sweep. They've silenced everyone," he said.

By this point Montalbano's blood was boiling so hot with rage that he felt it pounding in his temples.

"Excuse me just a minute," he said.

And he went into the bathroom, turned on the tap, and put his head under the cold running water. Then he dried himself off and went back to Gambardella.

"There's no point wasting any more time here," he said brusquely. "I have to go to the office."

Gambardella stood up and followed him. They went outside, and got into their cars. Gambardella shot off like a rocket, but the inspector's car started up and then immediately stalled. He started it up again, and it stalled again. There wasn't a drop of petrol in the tank. Luckily he kept a small jerry can in the boot.

He opened the car door, and just as he was getting out, the heavens opened and released an avalanche of water. In the twinkling of an eye, he was soaked.

As he was putting the petrol in the tank, he realized he needed to change his clothes. He cursed like a madman during the entire operation. Then he went back into the house, ran into the kitchen, grabbed a dish and hurled it against the wall, shattering it. Then a second, and a third.

At last he felt a little calmer.

He changed his clothes and went out again.

Fazio already knew about Pennisi's murder.

"They've screwed us, Chief."

And you don't even know that Asciolla has run away, Montalbano thought to himself.

But he said:

"No, I don't think so. But it'll all depend on what you tell me."

"Where should I start?"

"With whether, among the heads of the six companies, there's anyone who has anything, in one way or another, to do with the Cuffaros or the Sinagras."

"That one's easy. But I'll have to look at my notes."

"Then look."

Fazio took a piece of paper out of his pocket and consulted it.

"The whole thing's rather strange and complicated. Take Rosaspina, for example. We have Dr Filipepi, who is the Cuffaros' family doctor, on the board of directors."

"We already knew that."

"Yeah. But I've discovered that Barbera has defended the Sinagras twice in lawsuits."

"What are you saying? The Sinagras and Cuffaros, together in the same company?"

"That's right. And the same is true with Albachiara and Soledoro."

"Meaning there's always a friend of the Cuffaros and a friend of the Sinagras on the board of directors?"

"Correct."

"So what's the situation with the other firms?"

"The boards of Lo Schiavo, Spampinato, and Farullo haven't got anyone representing either the Cuffaros or the Sinagras. There was one name that caught my eye, however. *Ragioniere* Fasolo, who works for Spampinato."

"Why?"

"I'd heard talk of him but I couldn't remember where. Then it came back to me."

"Tell me."

"*Ragioniere* Fasolo was on the board of directors of Primavera when it went belly-up, but he was acquitted at the trial when Rosales, the president of the company, declined to implicate him. Now, I'd like to digress for a minute and talk about this Rosales . . ."

Damn, what a good policeman Fazio was!

"You can tell me about him later. There was something else I'd asked you about."

"You asked me whether Nicotra, when he worked for Primavera, had any assistants and, if so, where they'd ended up. Right?"

"Right."

"You must be speaking to the dead. Nicotra had two assistant accountants, named Foderaro and Giuffrida. Both are working today, Foderaro for Lo Schiavo and Giuffrida for Farullo. And each one has been promoted to chief accountant."

"And do you know where the accountants for Albachiara and Soledoro come from?"

Fazio looked at him in admiration. Damn, what a good policeman his boss was!

"Yes, I do. They come —"

"Wait, don't tell me. Let me try and guess. They come from Primavera."

"You're wrong, but not by much. They come from 21st of March, which was a firm —"

"— set up by Rosales."

Fazio rebelled.

"But you're just making me jump through hoops!"

"Why do you say that?"

"Well, if you already know all about Rosales . . ."

"I assure you that I didn't know the first thing about him until yesterday evening."

The inspector paused, got up, went over to the window, and opened it. He lit a cigarette, took three drags, threw it out, closed the window, and sat down again.

"Do you realize what we've discovered?" he asked.

"I'm starting to get an idea, but it's probably better if you tell me."

"You've confirmed my suspicions."

"And what were they?"

"That these six companies represent an agreement between the Vigàtese Mafia and the Trapanese Mafia. And that their mutual surveillance was assured by installing their respective representatives on each of the different boards of directors. An intersecting surveillance."

"That doesn't really make sense."

"Why not?"

"Because, just to take one example, there's no representative of Rosales on the board of Rosaspina."

"Yes, but there was Nicotra, as chief accountant. And you should pay close attention to something you said."

"What?"

"That everyone handling the money in those six firms are Rosales's people."

"And what does that mean?"

"It means that if the others are all chief accountants, he, Rosales, is the big chief of all the chief accountants."

"So, if that's the way it is, the capital behind the six companies is all his?"

"Are you kidding? In your opinion, would the Cuffaros and Sinagras ever put themselves in a subordinate position to Rosales?"

"Never. But then I wonder: how is it that when Rosales won the contract for Primavera, they waged war on him and won, and now they're hand in glove with him?"

"Apparently when Rosales was in gaol, or just out, he had one of his typically brilliant ideas and discussed it with his enemies. And he persuaded them to come to an agreement. Which worked fine until somebody broke into Nicotra's house. The break-in, the death of Nicotra, the kidnapping of Inge and her supposed uncle shattered a balance. And Rosales ordered his playmates in high places to impose a stop on everything until things get settled."

"But we still don't know who ordered the break-in or why. Total darkness."

"Right."

"And the agreement we've discovered is of no use to us outside these four walls, because we have no proof whatsoever."

"Right."

The telephone rang.

"Chief, 'at'd be Prossecator Giacono onna line an' 'e wants a talk —"

"Put him through," said Montalbano, turning on the speakerphone.

"Jacono here. I wanted to inform you that one of the inmates who took part in the brawl this morning has sung. The whole scuffle was started by a certain Renato Pusateri, who was the one that killed Pennisi."

"Do you know why Pusateri's in gaol?"

"Blackmail and attempted murder."

The inspector thanked the prosecutor and hung up.

"Why did you pull a face when you heard Pusateri's name?" he asked Fazio.

"Because I know who he is."

"And who is he?"

"One of the Sinagras' hirelings."

"So it all adds up. The proof is in the pudding. The Cuffaros find the scapegoat and the Sinagras kill him."

"So, what's our next move?"

"In my opinion, something has to happen before the day is out. Something that would fundamentally confirm what I'm thinking."

"*O matre santa!* Another murder?"

"No, on the contrary. It'll be good news. Shall we make a bet?"

"Nah, Chief, I never bet against you."

"Well, I'll tell you anyway. Before this evening, we'll get news that the regional administration has lifted the stoppage at the building sites."

"And what will that mean?"

"It'll mean they've recovered their balance and that, with Pennisi dead, they have nothing more to fear."

"But there's still Inge who —"

"Inge and the uncle they killed off some time ago — that, I'm sure of. Too dangerous to let live. They'd seen and heard too much. And, whatever the case, as far as Inge's concerned, they've covered themselves by making us think she's alive in Germany."

"OK, fine, but can you explain to me what good the reopening of the building sites will do for the investigation?"

"None at all, at least not directly. But indirectly, it will do some good. I'll explain. Do you also know that Rosales has been ill for months, is under house arrest, and refuses to see anyone?"

"Yeah, I knew that."

"We know, however, that Rosales hasn't stopped conducting his little business deals, right?"

"Right."

"Therefore, we know he hasn't had any direct contact with people. Are you with me?"

"I'm with you."

"So how does he communicate with the six companies?"

"By telephone."

"Right you are."

"Do you want to have it tapped?"

"Right again."

Fazio made his usual negative grimace.

"You don't agree?"

"I do."

"What is it, then?"

"No prosecutor will ever give you authorization."

"Whoever mentioned asking for authorization?"

Fazio opened his eyes wide.

"Are you joking?"

"No."

"Chief, do you want to end up in prison?"

Augello came in, but seeing Fazio and the inspector deeply involved in their discussion, he said nothing and sat down.

"If you think you can just tap Rosales —"

"Fucking hell!" Augello suddenly shouted, springing to his feet.

CHAPTER
SEVENTEEN

"What's the matter with you?" Montalbano asked in shock.

Fazio just stared at him in astonishment.

Mimì didn't answer, but only beamed a smile midway between imbecilic and beatific.

Outside, the storm went wild at that exact moment, the lightning flashing continuously. Amidst the pandemonium, Mimì started dancing around the room as though snakebitten, muttering:

"I'm free! I'm free! I was going crazy!"

Montalbano shot to his feet, grabbed him by the shoulders, and forced him to return to his seat.

"Free of what?" he asked.

"I'm free of my obsession with the name of the tattooed man I couldn't remember. It's Rosales!"

Fazio made some sort of exclamation that remained incomprehensible.

"Are you sure?" the inspector asked loudly, grabbing him forcefully by the lapels with both hands and practically shaking him. "Are you really, positively, absolutely sure? Eh?"

"Absolutely certain! And take your hands off me!"

"Oh. Sorry," said the inspector, letting him go and sitting back down behind his desk.

Then he asked:

"Do you remember where you saw him?"

Augello answered decisively.

"At the Fiacca Yacht Club. It was summertime, and he'd just gone for a swim. The girl I was with introduced us. Rosales was the club's vice-president."

A flash brighter than the rest burst into the dark room with a light as powerful as the sun.

But neither Fazio nor Augello saw it, because the flash had occurred only inside the inspector's head.

"Thanks to you, Mimì," he said after a pause, "the investigation can now proceed down the right path. We finally know that the man Inge said was her uncle was in fact Rosales. And this discovery partly confirms what I'd been starting to think, and partly sheds new light on things. Pennisi was lying as usual when he said he heard him speaking German. The only one who told us the truth about Rosales was the miserable Pitrineddru."

"But why did he always wear gloves?" Augello asked. "I can't work it out."

"Because his fingerprints were taken, as is the rule, when he was sent to prison for the Primavera fraud. And so he was wearing gloves as a precaution. At Nicotra's he was supposed to keep out of sight. And it was supposed to look as if he'd never even been there."

"From what I was able to find out, Rosales was under house arrest. Which means daily checks. So how was he able to move in with the Nicotras?" Fazio asked.

"He hadn't been under house arrest for a while. Gambardella said it was only until six months ago. And so, once out from under his surveillance and a free citizen again, he moved into Nicotra's house — still on the sly, of course, and still pretending he was deathly ill at his own home in Sicudiana."

"But why would he do that?" asked Augello.

"Here we enter the realm of conjecture. And I'll tell you my hunch. Actually, my conviction. It's not a certainty, but a conviction. Clear?"

"Clear," said the other two.

"Fazio, write this all down, would you? I'll need it when I go and talk to Jacono. Now listen carefully. The origin of the whole affair is to be found when Rosales wins the contract for the water main for Primavera."

"Which is in fact a sort of declaration of war on the Mafia families here," Fazio observed.

"And indeed one wonders how he managed to win such a contract on turf that the Cuffaro and Sinagra families control, right down to the sale of chicory. There can only be one answer: Rosales has very important political friends in the regional administration."

"Starting with the Public Works Council," said Fazio, "which by all appearances always falls in line."

"But the Cuffaros and Sinagras," Montalbano resumed, "cannot tolerate this loss of money and, more importantly, of prestige, and they do and say everything in their power so that charges are brought against Primavera, who are forced to shut things down. There's a trial and Rosales is convicted for the first time in his life, though he gets off with a light sentence. Everything clear, so far?"

"Perfectly," the two responded in unison.

"Prison brings counsel, however, and inside his cell —"

"No, Chief, because of his heart condition he was staying in the infirmary," Fazio pointed out.

"Well, let's just say that while in prison, Rosales has time to think about what has transpired and, like the intelligent man he is, realizes that instead of always making war on the Cuffaros and Sinagras, it would be better to have them as allies. But how can he do this? Turning the thought over in his mind, he gets a brilliant idea. And as soon as he's back home in Sicudiana, where he's still under house arrest, he finds a way to establish contact with his enemies and tells them about his plan. Which is so ingenious that the Cuffaros and Sinagras not only find themselves sharing the same thoughts without shooting each other, but in the end they embrace it."

"Well, tell the rest of us what it is!" Augello said impatiently.

"Rosales's brilliant idea has three critical points. The first is to create six companies that pretend to be in competition with one another but in reality are not, because they are secretly all connected. And they win all the public works contracts for Montelusa, Trapani, and respective provinces, eliminating any possibility for other companies to have a shot at these contracts."

"Just a minute," Augello interrupted him. "It doesn't seem to make much sense for the Sinagras and —"

"Just hold your horses, Mimì. Now to the second critical point. The lack of any actual competition automatically enables the six firms to greatly influence the rules of the different competitions. Not only that, but Rosales can count on superficial inspections from the regional administration, with the result that the six firms can use materials inferior to those stipulated in the contracts. Take the case of Albachiara and the school complex that started falling apart just a few months after it was opened. Convinced so far?"

"Fairly," said Augello. "But it seems to me that, whatever the case, the Cuffaros and Sinagras still end up losing a little of their autonomy, even though they gain a lot."

"And you can be sure they made this same argument to themselves," the inspector admitted. "But the third critical point of Rosales's plan overcomes any doubt. It is totally new but without any of the risks of novelty. Do you remember what Fort Knox was?"

"Wasn't that the fortress where all the gold reserves of the United States were kept?" said Fazio.

"That's right," Montalbano resumed. "As everybody knows, the problem with money earned illegally is that it has to be laundered. It starts out dirty and has to be cleaned. Some people take it out of the country, at great risk, some chop it up into very small chunks and turn it over to loan sharks and 'lenders' who hang out outside casinos, and so on. Rosales, on the other hand, suggests that they keep everyone's money on the 'premisses', as Catarella would say, to avoid all danger of transporting it, and then launder it, still locally, in the form of cash payments to the construction workers. And this turns out to be the winning idea."

"And in fact . . ." Fazio said thoughtfully. "It's my understanding that the workers are paid in cash."

"Mine, too," said Montalbano. And he continued: "Rosales, as the brains behind the whole set-up, can lay claim to two and a half companies — namely all of Albachiara and Soledoro, and half of Rosaspina, the other half of which goes in equal parts to the Cuffaros and the Sinagras, who also own three companies: that is, Spampinato, Lo Schiavo, and Farullo. Everything clear to you guys?"

"Perfectly," said Fazio.

"To continue. Once the agreement is approved, the Cuffaros and Sinagras see to the construction — by men they trust absolutely — of the basement with the safe under the garage beside the house lived in by Nicotra, another trusted man of theirs. That safe will become the depository of all the cash taken in by the three gangs and in need of laundering. Now you have to consider the fact that this safe had to be opened at least one day a week, to remove the money owed to the employees of the six different firms."

"Do you have any idea who the cashier could have been?" Mimì asked, with interest, at this point.

"Of course," Montalbano replied. "That, in fact, was Rosales's job, and that's why he moved in with the Nicotras. And to avoid any unpleasant surprises, he brought along, with his gloves and heart medicine, two nasty revolvers, one for him, and the other for the man of the house. All the accountants of the six firms are

Rosales's men, and they know how to proceed. Business was going swimmingly until something happened that sent the whole system's balance up in smoke."

"You mean the break-in?"

"Exactly."

"And who was it, in your opinion?"

"Nicotra himself gave me a lead."

"What?" Augello asked in amazement.

"By going and dying inside the Rosaspina tunnel. He was sending us a message: *This* is where you must look for the motive. Right here. And in fact Rosaspina is the only one of those firms where Rosales had no representative on the board of directors, aside from Nicotra himself, who was the chief accountant. I am more than convinced that the only people who could have taken the money and kidnapped Rosales are either the Cuffaros or the Sinagras. There's just no getting around it."

"But why do you say that?" asked Augello.

"Because, in my opinion, there was some sort of dispute over the sharing of the profits of Rosaspina. There is no other explanation. Putting the Cuffaros and Sinagras together is like putting the devil and holy water together. The stupidest little thing would suffice to set the demons loose. Then, during the kidnapping — which was supposed to happen under wraps, unbeknownst to anyone, with no bloodshed, and only to strengthen their position — somebody gets killed. And this puts the whole operation at risk. As a first step, the regional politicians with a stake in the affair, after much hand-wringing, impose a work stoppage on all six sites. The Cuffaros, or the Sinagras, are then forced to free Rosales, who goes back to his home in Sicudiana, to return the money, and to clear up the murder. So they send us Pennisi. That way the whole incident is over, and everyone can go back to work."

"And what about Inge?" Augello asked.

"Inge, as I've already told Fazio, had to be eliminated out of necessity. You can't let someone who knows everything live. One word from her would have been enough to send the whole operation to the dogs."

He got up, went and drank some water, then sat down again. The storm outside was moving away.

"Take my notes," said Fazio, handing them to him. Montalbano put them in his jacket pocket.

"What do you think you'll do?" asked Augello.

"Right now I'm going to call Jacono and find out whether he'll see me this afternoon."

Mimì twisted up his mouth.

"I don't think you'll succeed."

"You don't?"

"The story you just told is straight out of a good Mafia novel. You have no proof of anything."

"You're right. We'll have to start looking for proof."

"How?"

"If Rosales has gone back to Sicudiana, and I'm convinced he has, how does he get in touch with the others? I want authorization to tap his phones and put him under video and audio surveillance."

"Best of luck," said Augello, getting up and leaving the room.

Fazio was pensive.

"Tell me what's going through your head, Fazio."

"I was thinking that there's a carabinieri station at Sicudiana where a friend of mine works, Corporal Giammarco. I want to call him."

"To ask him something?"

"You can be sure they keep an eye on Rosales, right?"

"Right."

"So I want to know if anything concerning Rosales has happened in the past few days."

"OK, you try and talk to him while I call Jacono."

The prosecutor gave him an appointment for three o'clock. Fazio came back fifteen minutes later.

"Giammarco told me that about a week ago — he can't remember exactly when — the doctor in charge of Rosales was summoned one night for an emergency, and for three days didn't budge from his bedside."

"It tallies," said Montalbano. "He must have been unwell after the kidnapping and needed urgent care as soon as he got back home. With the heart condition he's got . . ."

It was raining lightly when he went out to eat. Entering the trattoria, he sat down at his usual place, and the television was on. Enzo, knowing that it bothered the inspector, turned it off.

"Any interesting news?" Montalbano asked.

"They said the regional administration has lifted the stoppage order from all six building sites, so work can resume. At least I don't have to worry about my brother-in-law any more."

As we were saying . . .

This was the latest confirmation of the inspector's hypothesis.

A mighty hunger came over him. He would completely stuff himself. But then the thought that he wouldn't be able to take a digestive walk out to the lighthouse, because he had to see Jacono, held him back.

It was going to be a difficult meeting. Wouldn't it be best to go there fortified?

No, the way of wisdom is always the middle path.

"Shall I bring you some antipasti?"

"No. Have you got spaghetti in squid ink today?"

"Yes."

"Bring me a large portion."

"As a second course I've got stone bass à la 'Sposito."

"Who's this 'Sposito?"

"A Neapolitan cook who taught me how to make the sauce."

"What's it like?"

"At first it tastes sweet, but underneath it all it's sour. It's a sauce you could say is misleading."

"OK."

It may have been thanks to the sauce that he emerged from the restaurant in a combative spirit.

Since he had the time, he didn't drive straight to Montelusa but took a detour by way of Riguccio.

The Albachiara building site was still empty. Work would resume the following day. Before Montalbano's eyes lay a sea of mud in which the landscape itself was drowning. But because of all the storms there had been, the pyramid of mud had lost its peak.

It was a decapitated pyramid. A ziggurat.

He took this as a good omen.

He waited a while in the car, going over the notes Fazio had taken. Then he drove off.

Jacono sat and listened to him attentively for a good hour and more without once interrupting him.

And he didn't open his mouth even after the inspector had finished talking.

So Montalbano, feeling impatient, prodded him.

"Aren't you going to say anything?"

"I'm sorry, I was just thinking."

Moments later he sighed and shook his head.

Montalbano spoke again.

"Tell me sincerely whether —"

"Montalbano, everything you've told me makes perfect sense. It's all well founded and logical, but, you see . . ."

"I see what?"

"There are so many things."

"Tell me one."

"Well, just to cite the first example that comes to mind, the accusations you level at the regional council . . ."

"I get it. The usual special consideration for politics."

Jacono slammed his hand down on the desk and said angrily:

"I don't grant special consideration to anyone! And you should think twice before you talk like that to me!"

Montalbano bit his tongue and restrained himself. That wasn't the right approach to take with Jacono.

"I apologize," he muttered.

"Let's both of us calm down. What I meant to say was that these are grave accusations unsupported by so much as a shred of proof. Do you realize this?"

"Of course."

"Then tell me how you would proceed."

"By decapitating the pyramid."

"I don't understand."

"By making it possible for you to charge Rosales."

"All right, but how?"

"If I had authorization to tap his phone and put him under video and audio surveillance . . ."

"Rosales?"

"Yes."

"Montalbano, put yourself in my shoes for a minute. I have to account for and justify every action I take to my superiors. How will I explain that kind of surveillance? You haven't given me a single scrap of evidence, do you realize that?"

"I have a witness who saw Rosales in Nicotra's house — at a time when he had everyone believing he was at home in Sicudiana."

"Well, that might be something . . . Is he a solid witness?"

Montalbano had a moment of doubt. Could one rely on Pitrineddru? That big ape of a man? No, a good lawyer would eat him alive.

"Unfortunately, no. He's a bit off in the head."

"Well, then, for now it's best not to bring him into this. Got any other cards in your hand?"

"Unfortunately, no."

Jacono threw his arms in the air.

"I don't know how to proceed in the eyes of the law."

"So we have to drop the whole thing?"

Jacono looked him straight in the eye.

"I didn't mean that. I only said that I, as public prosecutor, don't know how to proceed in the eyes of the law. But you, as a police inspector, can perhaps view the question in a different light."

Did he understand correctly what the prosecutor was suggesting to him? He wanted to be sure.

"Maybe I —"

"A few minutes ago," Jacono cut in, not letting him finish, "you used a certain word, 'pyramid', which brought to mind . . . Did you know that for a very long time nobody could go inside the Pyramid of Cheops because nobody knew where the entrance was? Then someone took the bull by the horns and bored a hole into the wall, without the authorization of the pyramid's custodians. Now, though, the custodians, who until that moment had no way of entering, could also go inside."

What a bastard this Jacono was! In effect he was saying: *If you can manage to pull something off that's not strictly in keeping with the law, then be my guest.*

They exchanged a warm goodbye.

After leaving the courthouse, he went to the nearest cafe, sat down at a table, and ordered a whisky.

His brain was whirring like a propeller on an aeroplane. What could he do, apart from surveillance, to find evidence against Rosales?

The only hope was to lay a trap for him. To set up a ruse that he would take to be real.

But how?

Nothing came to him.

He ordered another whisky.

A well-dressed lady came in. She peeled off a glove and was about to put it down on the table next to the inspector's when it fell to the floor.

Montalbano bent down, picked it up, and . . .

. . . remained just like that, as though paralysed, frozen.

"Are you going to give me back my glove?" the woman asked impatiently.

Montalbano gave it back to her, got up, went over to the cash register, paid for his whiskies, pulled out his mobile phone, and dialled Jannaccone's number.

"Montalbano here."

"What can I do for you, Inspector?"

"If I drop by in about fifteen minutes, who will I run into, you or your boss?"

"You'll run into me."

"I'm on my way."

CHAPTER
EIGHTEEN

Fifteen minutes later he was in Jannaccone's office.

"If I remember correctly, you guys found two pairs of cotton gloves in the dustbin at Nicotra's house."

"Yes. We've classified them as exhibits."

"Did you get any fingerprints from them?"

"Of course. But there were so many superimposed on one another that they were illegible."

"Could you lend me them for two days?"

"No problem."

Getting back in the car, he looked at his watch. It was five-thirty. Just to be safe, he rang Catarella.

"Are Augello and Fazio on the premises?"

"Yeah, Chief, righ' 'ere onna premises."

"Tell them not to budge from the station for any reason until I get there."

Driving back to Vigàta, he drove faster than he ever had before. He wanted to put his plan into action that very evening. He was worried that the following day, after a night's sleep, the wisdom and caution of his age might advise him against it.

"Don't put any calls through to me, and get me Augello and Fazio," he said to Catarella upon entering the station.

"'Ey're awriddy onna premisses."

In fact they were standing by the window, chatting. As soon as they saw the inspector they approached.

"Did Jacono give you the authorization?" Augello asked hopefully.

"No. Have a seat, both of you."

He told them what had transpired with Jacono.

"Simply speaking, does this mean that we have to drop the investigation?"

"You two, yes. Me, no," said Montalbano.

They looked at each other, stunned.

"What does that mean?" Augello asked.

"It means I'm planning to lay a trap for Rosales. Without court authorization, mind you. For that reason, since such a thing could jeopardize your careers, I'm leaving you two out of it. Whereas me, since I've already gone as far as I'll go, I don't care. Clear?"

"Clear," said Augello.

"It's clear to me, too," said Fazio, "but, if possible, I'd like to know what this trap of yours consists of."

Montalbano explained it to him.

"There's one flaw," Augello observed.

"Namely?"

"You can't go alone. You wouldn't be believable. Anyway, what is this, a cowboy movie where the sheriff goes and rounds up the bandits all by himself?"

239

Mimì was right. But the inspector didn't want to waste any time.

"I'm going anyway," he said. Then, turning to Fazio: "Explain to me how to get to Rosales's house in Sicudiana."

Fazio told him.

"I'll see you guys later," said Montalbano, standing up.

Augello and Fazio also stood up and followed him down to the car park.

"This is where we say goodbye," Montalbano said after getting in the car.

"Goodbye, no way," said Augello. "You go on ahead, and we'll follow behind you, each in our own car."

"You two are staying here. That's an order!" Montalbano retorted angrily, getting out of the car.

"Save the order for your sister," Mimì replied.

Montalbano took a step towards him, which was enough to allow Fazio to bend down and grab the keys, which the inspector had already stuck in the ignition.

Montalbano caught this out of the corner of his eye and weighed his options. If he made a fuss, he would just waste more time. And he didn't have much at his disposal. So he gave in.

"All right," he said through clenched teeth.

Smiling apologetically, Fazio gave him back the keys.

They stopped at a petrol station on the outskirts of Sicudiana.

"OK, Fazio, now you go in front of us and take us to Rosales's house. Does he have any family living with him?"

"A thirty-year-old nephew who helps him out. But it's possible he's got the house watched over by his men. And we may find him in the company of a few friends."

"In that case we'll clear them out."

"But is it possible he doesn't even have a housekeeper?" asked Augello.

"He may have one he hires by the hour. Apparently Rosales doesn't want any extraneous ears about the house that might overhear when he has guests or talks on the phone. And now let's go. This is it, guys. The stakes are high. Keep cool, and don't speak unless I address you first."

They set off. Ten minutes later they were outside Rosales's little palazzo, which was in the upper part of town and gave onto a piazza with a church and a school. There wasn't a soul around.

There was an entryphone outside the front door. Montalbano rang. A male voice answered.

"Who is it?"

"Police!"

"The police? What do you want?"

"Open up and we'll tell you."

"Wait a second and I'll come downstairs."

Then, in one of the two panels of the double front door, a sort of tiny window, protected by a cast-iron grate, opened. A man looked out at them, then said:

"Put your documents in the hole."

Which consisted of a rectangular slot in the other panel, over which was a metal plaque with the word LETTERS. The three did as they were asked.

One half of the door opened and immediately closed again after they entered a vestibule.

Before them stood a young man of about thirty, tall and athletic, with a revolver stuck into the waistband of his trousers.

"Sorry about all the precautions. But the way things are these days . . ."

"Yes, it's just terrible," said the inspector. "You can't trust anyone any more, and there's no respect for anybody. And who are you?"

"I'm Mr Rosales's nephew. My name is Adolfo."

"Is your uncle at home?"

"Where else would he be? He hasn't set foot out of here for two and a half months. He couldn't even if he wanted to."

"Why not?"

"His heart condition's got a lot worse in the last few days."

"What happened? Overexertion?"

The young man looked a little ill at ease.

"Well . . . at his age . . ."

"I understand. Is he resting at present?"

"He's in an armchair watching TV."

"Could I speak with him?"

"I'm sorry, but you can't. It would be too exhausting for him. The doctor said no visitors."

"I have a search warrant and a warrant for the arrest of your uncle. Here," Montalbano bluffed, sticking his hand into his jacket pocket as if to take out the documents.

Upon hearing these words, the young man turned pale as a corpse and seemed paralysed.

In a flash Fazio stepped forward and snatched the gun from his waistband. The nephew seemed not even to notice.

"Show me the way," said the inspector.

They climbed a staircase, went down a corridor, and entered a sort of spacious bedroom with tasteful furnishings. But the air stank of medicines and sickness.

Rosales was sitting in an armchair in front of a television turned off. To his left was a small table with two telephones and six mobile phones. To his right was another small table with a bottle of water, a glass, and a great many boxes of medicines. He'd fallen asleep.

Adolfo lightly shook him by the shoulder. Rosales opened his eyes and looked at the three in astonishment.

One could see that he was truly unwell. Sickly yellow, hollow-eyed, unshaven, and breathing with difficulty. He said nothing. Montalbano was the first to speak.

"Emilio Rosales, I am placing you under arrest."

At first Rosales didn't make the slightest move, and did not react in any visible way.

"Are you kidding me?" he then asked, venturing a hint of a smile. "What am I accused of?"

"Money laundering, racketeering, suborning of contract competitions, and one other more serious charge, which —"

"Money laundering and racketeering? Me?" Rosales cut him off. "I'm a building developer! At the very most I might grant you the false — I repeat, false — accusation of suborning the competition, but as for the rest . . ."

"You don't know that we discovered the safe under Nicotra's garage," Montalbano blurted out.

Rosales absorbed the blow. He closed his eyes and shook his head, but quickly recovered.

"Of course I knew poor Nicotra, but I have no idea where he was living."

"You're making the wrong move, I'm warning you. Did you also know his wife, Inge Schneider?"

"I knew he had a good-looking German wife, but I never saw her."

"Second wrong move. We have an eyewitness who in his declaration to the prosecutor said he saw you as you were . . . ahem . . . intimately engaged with the woman in the room you were staying in at Nicotra's house."

The blow was harder this time. Rosales was overcome with a coughing fit, started gasping for breath, and didn't calm down until Adolfo got him to drink some water. Then he was in a condition to defend himself.

"So you came here to tell me a story straight out of the puppet theatre. But if you can't show me any proof . . ."

"Here you go," said the inspector, extracting from his jacket pocket two cellophane bags, each containing a pair of cotton gloves soiled from use.

"For the whole time you were staying at Nicotra's house as the . . . let's call it the cashier and guardian of the dirty money, you wore gloves like this to avoid leaving any fingerprints. But there are fingerprints inside the gloves — plenty of them! You should have burned them, not thrown them in the bin."

Rosales remained silent.

Montalbano suddenly heard bells ringing joyfully in his head. The trap was working to perfection.

He put the gloves back in his pocket and said:

"There's another decisive element that proves you were in that house. Your blood on the pillow, which got there when the assailants surprised you in bed and punched you in the face to make you get up and open the safe. We've recovered the DNA from that blood sample. You do realize you cannot deny the evidence, don't you?"

Again Rosales said nothing. His breathing had become so laboured that Fazio looked at Montalbano with concern.

"Do you want to summon the doctor?" Montalbano asked Adolfo.

"I think it would be best."

"Then call him."

Adolfo pulled out a mobile phone, spoke, then signed off. "He'll be right over."

"Mr Rosales," the inspector continued, "now listen to me carefully, because compared to what I'm about to say to you now, everything I've told you so far will seem like a joke."

"A joke?" said Rosales, eyes opening wide.

"You interrupted me while I was listing the charges."

"There are others?"

"Yes, complicity in the attempted murder of Saverio Piscopo and in the murders of Pino Pennisi and Inge Schneider."

Rosales reacted in a manner nobody was expecting. Making a desperate effort, he rose to his feet. He was shaking all over and had trouble speaking.

"I . . . had nothing . . . to do with those murders . . . it was the Cuffaros . . . who came and kidnapped me and took the money . . . They thought I was in league with the Sinagras to screw them . . ."

He fell back into the armchair, drained of strength. But Montalbano wasn't about to back off now.

"I am quite certain that the money momentarily stolen by the Cuffaros has been returned," he said, "and that the kitty is back in working order. But since there hasn't been enough time to set up a new underground bank, the prosecutor is convinced the money is here with you. And I have a search warrant signed by him. My question for you is: what if you saved me the time and just told me where it is?"

Rosales sat there a few moments before answering. Then he signalled to Adolfo to come near and with effort whispered something into his ear. Adolfo opened a small drawer in the table with the telephones and took out a key.

"The money is in an old wardrobe in the attic," said Adolfo. "I'll take you there myself."

"You go with him," the inspector said to Fazio.

As soon as the two left the room, the front door buzzer went.

"That must be the doctor," said Mimì. "I'll let him in."

Then, as soon as Montalbano was left alone with Rosales, something happened that took Montalbano completely by surprise.

Rosales opened his eyes and smiled at him.

Montalbano was taken aback.

Then Rosales said something the inspector didn't get.

He gestured to him to come closer.

"Just between us, man to man . . . it was all a ruse, right?"

"What was?"

"The fingerprints . . . the DNA . . . all that nonsense you told me . . . It's true I was the cashier and the guardian . . . and I'll tell that to the judge, don't worry . . . but you didn't have any proof . . . You just conned me. Am I right? You must tell me!"

Montalbano preferred answering indirectly, and he abandoned all pretence of formality.

"So then, if you knew, why did you fall for it anyway?"

"First of all because I'm tired, and second because you're giving me a good opportunity to get even with those dickhead Cuffaros."

Mimì came in with the doctor, who took one look at Rosales and started to worry.

"Please leave the room," he said to Montalbano and Augello.

The two went out into the corridor, where they ran into Fazio and Adolfo returning from the attic.

"At a glance I'd say there's about thirty million up there, in a green wardrobe," said Fazio.

He gave the inspector the key, which he put in his pocket.

"Phone Catarella and tell him to send Gallo with three men," said Montalbano. "We need to keep a watch on Rosales and all this money."

He walked a few steps down the corridor to call Jacono.

"I'm sorry to disturb you, sir, but you need to come to Sicudiana at once to take Rosales's confession. Among other things, there's about thirty million euros in cash still waiting to be laundered."

"How on earth did you manage that?" Jacono asked in astonishment.

"I took your advice. I made a hole in the side of the pyramid."

He told him how to get to Rosales's house and then hung up.

The doctor came out of the bedroom and Montalbano approached him.

"How is he?"

"Bad, very bad. He told me he's under arrest, but it's my duty to tell you that Mr Rosales can't be moved."

"I imagined as much. Not even in an ambulance?"

"Not even in an ambulance. I put him back to bed, and he must not move from there."

"I beg you please to do me a favour. In half an hour at the most, the prosecutor will be here to interrogate

248

him, so there won't be any need to move him from his bed. Could you stay for the questioning, in case he needs help?"

"It's my duty."

The doctor turned away to go back into the bedroom.

Montalbano followed him.

"What else do you want?" the doctor asked gruffly.

Montalbano didn't answer. He moved the doctor aside and went in. Rosales was lying down but had his eyes open.

"I wanted to inform you that Prosecutor Jacono will be here shortly to take your deposition."

Rosales twisted up his mouth.

"He's a tough one, I know," the inspector continued. "Would you like me to summon your lawyer? It's your right. Just give me his name and phone number and —"

Rosales didn't have to think twice.

"Forget about the lawyer. After all, in my present situation, one lawyer more, one lawyer less . . . Thanks, anyway, and goodbye."

"Goodbye," said Montalbano. And he left.

"I'm going outside to smoke a cigarette," he said to Fazio and Augello.

He leaned against the door to keep it open, and started smoking. He felt relieved. It had all been a lot easier than he'd expected. All the same, he had a slightly bitter taste in his mouth. One question still bothered him. If Rosales hadn't felt like walking into the trap, how would things have turned out?

He looked at his watch. Almost half-past eight. The whole thing looked like it was going to take a while, so he'd better call Livia.

"Hi, how are you?"

"Pretty good. But if only you were here . . ."

"I will be there," he said. "Tomorrow."

The words had slipped out of his mouth before he could stop them.

He could feel Livia holding her breath.

"Do you really mean that?"

"I really mean it. I'll be at your place by the end of the day."

"God, how wonderful! You have no idea how much . . ."

"What are you doing? Crying?"

"Yes, and I'm not ashamed to say it. I lo —"

Better change the subject.

"Tell me about Selene."

"She's such a little troublemaker . . ."

The siren of an approaching car drowned her out.

"I'm sorry, but I have to go. Hugs and kisses. See you tomorrow."

Gallo's car arrived like a rocket and screeched to a halt about a foot away from the inspector, who for a second feared he was going to end up squashed on the pavement.

"OK, you three get out, go inside, and make yourselves available to Inspectors Augello and Fazio.

You, Gallo, park the car properly and then go and join the others."

Montalbano felt like breathing the open air, not the stale air of rooms in which illness reigned. When Gallo came up beside him, the inspector said to him: "Tell Inspector Augello to come out here."

Mimì arrived on the run.

"What is it?"

"I just wanted to inform you that I'll be dropping in at the station early tomorrow morning, but I won't be staying. I'll be leaving again immediately."

"When'll you be back?"

"In about a week."

Augello was stunned.

"What? At a time like this?"

"Yes, at a time like this. What's the point in hanging around?"

"Jacono might need you!"

"You'll be here. If the worst comes to the worst, he can ring me in Genoa."

At that moment a fast car pulled up, and Jacono and another man who must have been the clerk of the court got out. They shook hands with Montalbano and Augello.

"I'll show you the way," said the inspector.

It was past midnight by the time he got home. The interrogation of Rosales would resume the following morning. Fazio and the four other officers had stayed behind to guard the house. An armoured van would also be there the next morning to secure the money.

Montalbano opened the French windows. It had started raining ever so lightly.

His hunger had been so long neglected that Adelina's pasta and fish seemed to take for ever to warm up.

When he had finished, he went immediately to bed and plunged into an abyss of sleep.

At six the following morning he got up, packed his bag, phoned the police station at Punta Raisi airport, got them to reserve him a seat on the eleven o'clock flight, then got in his car, went to the office, wrote his request for a leave of absence, and left it with Catarella to give to HR.

Then he got back into the car and went to a supermarket with a pet-products department. He bought an artificial bone and a stuffed beaver that squeaked when you squeezed it. Selene was sure to love it.

Author's Note

This novel is entirely of my own invention, although it takes its cue from far too many almost-daily news stories of a similar subject.

I am nevertheless keen to state that this book contains no intentional reference to real living persons or situations that have actually happened, or to any existing political institutions.

A.C.

Notes

page 3 — ***purpiteddri a strascinasale***: baby octopus simmered in salt water and served simply with lemon and olive oil.

page 25 — **Finance Police:** Italy has a separate police bureaucracy called La Guardia di Finanza, whose principal responsibility is to enforce laws concerning fiscal matters.

page 44 — ***bunga bunga***: while the term is believed to originate in indigenous Australian culture, it gained popular currency in Italy around 2010, in reference to the wild sex parties purportedly held by controversial tycoon and Prime Minister Silvio Berlusconi. Opinions differ as to its exact meaning in this context, with some maintaining it refers to "an orgy with a powerful leader", and others claiming it involved underwater sex games between a nude host and a bevy of naked young women. Actress Sabina Began, a former mistress of Berlusconi's, claimed the term referred to parties she had organized, and that it was based on her name. Whatever the case, in common Italian parlance, *bunga*

bunga has come to refer to the dubious nature of the former Prime Minister's tastes in personal entertainment, especially after the scandal of his having had sexual relations, in exchange for money and career promotion, with an underage Moroccan girl.

page 54 — **What poetic names these firms had!:** the names Rosaspina, Albachiara, Soldedoro, and Primavera mean, respectively, "Rosethorn", "Bright Dawn", "Golden Sun", and "Springtime".

page 62 — **Boccadasse:** the suburb of Genoa where Livia lives.

page 72 — **"When have us police ever woiked t'getter with the carabinieri?":** the competition, in Italy, between the carabinieri — a national police force with broad, almost universal jurisdiction and a division of the army — and the local police forces, the Commissariati di Pubblica Sicurezza, of which Montalbano's unit is one, is the stuff of legend. The carabinieri are also often the butt of nationwide jokes.

page 73 — *sartù:* a hearty Neapolitan dish that is basically a savoury cake filled with rice, *ragù* sauce, cheese (usually mozzarella), meatballs, sausages and chicken livers.

page 76 — *"E lucean le stelle . . .":* known usually with the more modern imperfect tense of the verb ("E lucevan le stele"), this is the famous melancholy aria

("And the stars were shining") from Act III of Puccini's *Tosca*, sung by Cavaradossi while a prisoner at the Castel Sant'Angelo in Rome, awaiting execution.

page 142 — **The Pizza Triangle** (orig. title, *Dramma della gelosia*): a madcap 1970 tragicomedy by Ettore Scola, starring Marcello Mastroianni, Monica Vitti and Giancarlo Giannini, featuring an ill-fated love triangle in which the two rivals fighting for the beautiful Vitti's attentions end up accidentally killing her.

page 159 — **the prefect:** unlike the French *préfet*, who is a sort of police commissioner, in Italy, the *prefetto* is a local bureaucratic representative of the authority of the national government.

page 162 — **"Nobody makes it to a thousand euros a week anyway.":** in an attempt to reduce tax fraud in Italy, a few years ago it became illegal to make any payments of one thousand euros or more in cash.

page 211 — *"È primavera, svegliatevi bambine . . .":* "It's spring! Wake up, little girls!"

Notes by Stephen Sartarelli

Other titles published by Ulverscroft:

A NEST OF VIPERS

Andrea Camilleri

On what should be a quiet Sunday morning, Inspector Montalbano is called to a murder scene on the Sicilian coast. A man has discovered his father dead in his Vigàtan beach house: his body slumped on the dining-room floor, his morning coffee spilt across the table, and a single gunshot wound at the base of his skull. First appearances point to the son having the most to gain from his father's untimely death, a notion his sister can't help but reinforce. But when Montalbano delves deeper into the case, and learns of the dishonourable life the victim led, it soon becomes clear that half of Vigàta has a motive for his murder, and this won't be as simple as the inspector had once hoped . . .

THE WINGS OF THE SPHINX

Andrea Camilleri

Things are not going well for Inspector Salvo Montalbano. His long-distance relationship with Livia is on the rocks, his age is catching up with him, and he's getting tired of the violence that is part of his job. Then the dead body of a young woman is found. Her identity is at first unknown, but the tattoo of a sphinx moth on her left shoulder links her with three other girls bearing the same mark who have been rescued from the Mafia nightclub circuit by a prominent Catholic charity. The problem is, they can't help Montalbano with his enquiries — as they are all missing . . .

THE TRACK OF SAND

Andrea Camilleri

Inspector Salvatore Montalbano wakes one morning to find a gruesomely bludgeoned horse carcass in front of his seaside home — but when his men come to investigate, it has disappeared, leaving only a trail in the sand. Soon Rachele Esterman, a beautiful and wealthy equestrian, turns up at police headquarters to report her horse missing; it had been stabled on grounds belonging to Saverio Lo Duca, one of the richest men in Sicily — who, it emerges, lost one of his own horses at the same time. His curiosity piqued, Montalbano takes up the case, but things take a disturbingly personal turn with a series of mysterious break-ins at his house. Who has the inspector upset within the strange, glittering world of horse racing and the Mafia?

THE TREASURE HUNT

Andrea Camilleri

When a letter arrives containing a mysterious riddle, Inspector Montalbano becomes drawn into a perplexing treasure hunt set by an anonymous challenger. As the hunt intensifies, Montalbano is offered assistance from Arturo Pennisi, a young man eager to witness the detective's investigative skills first hand. Fending off meddling commissioners and his irate girlfriend, Livia, the inspector will follow the treasure hunt's clues and travel from Vigàta's teeming streets to its deserted outskirts. But when a horrifying crime is committed, the game must surely be laid aside. And it isn't long before Montalbano himself will be in terrible danger . . .